Thistles

Thistles

ɵ ɵ ɵ

a novella by

Kate McNeil

Twintype Books

Copyright Information

Thistles
by Kate McNeil

Dedication

This story is dedicated to indie authors and the readers who support them.

Table of Contents

Chapter One

Destroying someone's life could be remarkably cathartic.

It was a thought I turned over in my mind as the night slipped slowly by, comfortable and warm on the deep soft couch in, what had been up until very recently, Parker and Shane's apartment. Now it was just Parker's apartment, and if Shane had any brain cells whatsoever, he'd cut his losses and be glad that we'd only tossed his stuff in the apartment complex dumpster without lighting it on fire first.

I sighed a little, pulling the heavy quilt that Gran had made while she was pregnant with Sarah, Parker's mom, higher up around my shoulders. Parker had of course offered to share the king-size bed in the apartment's one bedroom, but I told her that I'd be tossing and turning all night, and didn't want to keep her awake. I could see the questions she wanted to ask reflected in the eyes that knew me inside and out, but as such, she knew better than to push me. Instead she created a warm welcoming nest for me to snuggle into, then gave me a long hard hug before heading to bed.

I could tell that the quilt had been lovingly and carefully stored away in a linen closet: the smell of the lavender sachet that Sarah Chase had grown, dried and sewn herself was faint but undeniable as it surrounded me.

1

It was like a ghostly hug that gave me permission to cry a little more, even though each tear was like a drop of acid burning my heart away. I sealed the contents of the past few years firmly behind locks and keys that were melted into something cold and gray, taking up residence in the farthest corner of my heart.

Parker and I sat at the kitchen table the next morning, looking like survivors of the zombie apocalypse. I hadn't slept much at all and, from the looks of her, Parker hadn't either. We sipped our coffee silently, lost in our own thoughts, until a brisk knock at the door shook both of us out of our stupor. Parker shuffled over to unlock it, admitting the tiniest tornado in South Carolina.

"Well there you are, I was starting to...Vivian! Oh my stars! Oh my..." In the next second, I was wrapped in Gran's arms. Just like being under the quilt the night before, I felt another piece of myself come back home.

"Hi, Gran."

"Oh sweetpea, I just...why didn't you...oh my goodness!" Seeing Gran this flustered was rare, and Parker was grinning as she came back over and picked up her coffee cup.

"Surprise!"

"Parker, did you know she was coming home?"

"No, Gran, I swear I didn't."

"It was a last minute kind of thing." I smiled down

at the woman who had loved, scolded and spoiled both of us our entire lives. She may have been only Parker's grandmother biologically, but she was Gran to both of us.

"Well hallelujah, I was starting to think the army didn't grant leaves anymore and that we'd never see you again! How long are you in town for?"

Only years of practice kept the pain her question prompted from showing on my face. "I'm actually home for good."

I saw Parker's head snap up out of the corner of my eye, but I kept my focus on Gran.

"For good...oh my...Vivian Carmichael, you're going to make me cry! We've missed you so much!"

"I've missed you too."

"I was coming over to ask Parker and Shane if they'd like to come over for dinner tonight, but since you're home, I'll make all of your favorites!"

Parker cleared her throat. "Yeah, ah, about Shane..."

Gran swung around to face her, blinked, and then threw her hands up in the air. "Oh double hallelujah, you finally kicked that no-good bastard to the curb, didn't you?"

I couldn't help the snort of laughter that erupted from inside me. Parker crossed her arms. "Yep, kicked him to the curb, literally. All his stuff is in the dumpster out back. Unless he snuck back in the middle of the night to fish it out."

"This old lady's heart can only take so many wonderful surprises, this is like Christmas ten times over. Good riddance to bad rubbish."

"I didn't know you hated him, Gran."

"Well, as long as he made you happy, he was fine, dearie." Prim Gran was back. "But he hasn't made you happy in a long, long time. We could all see that. But it wasn't our place to tell you so."

"For future reference, feel free to tell me so. Would you like some coffee?"

"No thank you, I'm on my way to the market, they've got crab legs on sale and I've got to get there before they run out. But I'll expect you both at my house at 5pm sharp." She turned around and wrapped me in another tight hug. "Vivian, I'm so happy you're home. We've missed you so, so much. Please don't leave us ever again."

Another stab of pain that I forced down. The CIA had made it very clear I wouldn't be leaving the country for at least three years, so that was one promise I knew I could keep. "I won't."

"We'll catch up over dinner." She patted my cheek affectionately and then turned to wrap her granddaughter in an equally tight hug. "And if that no-good rat Shane comes sniffing around again..."

"Don't worry, I'll have Vivian put *him* in the dumpster out back."

"That's right. Well then, dearies, I'll see you in a little while!"

She bustled out the door, her entire visit lasting no more than a few minutes. When I turned to Parker, the smile on my face was finally genuine. "God I've missed her."

"Yeah, I didn't think it was possible, but she and I have been even closer since Mom died." Parker picked up our empty mugs and set them in the kitchen sink. "So...sounds like we've got a lot of catching up to do. Are we staying in or going out?"

"We're staying in because you need to call a locksmith and get the locks changed."

"Why do...oh. Oh yeah, good point." She gave me a crooked smile. "Back in town not even a day and you're already back to taking care of me."

"We take care of each other," I said firmly. "Listen, can I borrow an outfit for today? I'm going to need to go shopping, but that can wait."

"Yeah, of course." I knew she was dying of curiosity, considering I'd shown up at her apartment yesterday in a rumpled little black dress and carrying a couple of cheap bags I'd picked up at the airport. All of my clothes, along with boxes of jewelry, were literally a world away, hanging in a closet in Bulgaria. If they hadn't already erased all evidence that I'd ever been there.

"Thanks."

"No problem, grab whatever you want."

"I'm going to hop in the shower, you call a locksmith. Then, later," I took a deep breath, "Let's talk."

She nodded, knowing there was no further need for words between us. That connection we'd had since the day we were both born was as strong as though I hadn't been gone for years.

It was as strong as though I'd never been gone at all.

Living in Bulgaria hadn't changed my appreciation for Southern cuisine, and after the locksmith left, Parker and I headed to what had been our favorite seafood restaurant. Shane hated fish, so it was a treat for both of us.

It was right on the water, and a soft breeze stirred the salt-scented air around us, the sun warm on our shoulders. I hadn't realized I'd missed it so badly, and told Parker as much.

"I've always heard that travel will do that to you." We clinked glasses of sweet tea. "Here's to my best friend being home. And to her not leaving again."

I could hear the question in her words and took a deep breath, looking around the restaurant quickly. It was second nature. "Yeah, I'm home for good. I didn't leave under the best of circumstances."

Her eyes widened. "Are you okay?"

"Yes…and no." I looked around the restaurant again. "Something bad happened, so I'm no longer employed by them."

"And you had to leave so fast you couldn't even pack clothes?"

God she was sharp. "I didn't know I was coming back until I was on the way. But everything I had there…it was just stuff. I didn't have anything personal."

Our waiter came over with our appetizers and Parker smiled up at him, then waited before asking her next question. "Did you leave any*one*?"

My stomach churned with that one. "Yeah. I can't really talk about him just yet…"

"You don't have to tell me anything," she replied quickly. "I'm just worried about you. You look so different."

I played with my straw. "Well, I've been gone a long time. Almost eight years with only short little trips back."

"That's not what I mean." I could tell Parker was choosing her words carefully. "You look like you're in pain."

That was the understatement of the century. "His name is David," I finally said softly. "And he's the only regret I have…that they made me leave him behind too."

"Oh V," Parker wanted to hug me, but was trying to play it cool in public. "Is he…still there?"

I grinned a little. "I don't know. He could be sitting right here in this restaurant and we wouldn't know it."

She looked puzzled. "Well...whenever you want to talk about it, I'm here. Just let me know."

We intentionally changed the subject after that, and I felt myself slowly relaxing a little. Parker did most of the talking since I wasn't allowed to share the vast majority of what I'd been up to for the past few years.

"So the landlord's asshole son basically gave her six months' notice, which is insane. But Gran is taking it as a sign that maybe it's time to retire."

I shook my head. Black-Eyed Susans, Gran's flower shop, had been a Charleston institution for almost fifty years. "I can't imagine Gran retiring."

"Yeah, she can't either. Especially after Mom died, that shop has been her life. I used to have to kick her out so she could have a couple of days off, and I'd cover for her, but she's starting to do more social stuff. You'd be amazed at what senior citizens get up to in their ladies clubs."

"Well, that's good."

Parker shrugged. "It's funny how things line up...I'm going to be looking for a new job too. The company I work for is outsourcing a lot of their business, so they're laying a bunch of us off in a month. At least they were nice enough to give us a heads-up."

"So that's all three of us scanning the classified ads." I sighed and sat back in my chair. "I wonder if this is a sign from the universe."

"What do you mean?"

I shrugged. "All three of us needing gainful employment, and all three of us at a crossroads of sorts. I can't help but wonder if we should look at it as a hint that we should start fresh."

She perked up. "I'm game. Any suggestions?"

"After what we did to Shane's blog and email yesterday? We're meant to be hackers, obviously."

We both laughed. "That felt *so* good," Parker sighed. "Not just kicking his ass to the curb, in retrospect I should have done that a long time ago. But working with you, and seeing everything you had to teach me...that was *amazing*. I know it's nothing like what you...you know. But it was like putting together the biggest best Sodoku puzzle ever. I kinda want to do it again."

I smiled wistfully, knowing all too well how she felt. "Hey, I just provided the technical know-how, you did everything else."

"No way, no how. I literally just had a gut feeling, you did all the work."

"Someone had to teach me once too, you know."

"I wish the hacker thing was feasible," she laughed again. "I really enjoyed it."

"Now you know why I did what I did for so long."

"Oh yeah, totally. Was it really like that?"

"Uh, no. It's nothing like the movies. You'd be amazed how boring it can be at times. But when you're on a roll...yeah, there's nothing like it."

"Maybe you could do consulting work?" Parker suggested, finishing the last of her tea.

"I can't refer to my credentials, so that's out."

She frowned and I understood her confusion; anyone that hadn't signed their lives away didn't understand that I couldn't even acknowledge my employment, let alone use it as a reference. "You're not allowed to talk about it at all?"

"Nope." I played with the last of my entree. "It's a big black spot on my resume, which is going to make job-hunting a bit difficult."

"No time like the present for self-employment, then. I'd hire you."

I flicked my crumpled straw wrapper at her. "To do what?"

"You know, *spy stuff*." She mouthed the last two words. "You have the know-how, you should totally take advantage of it. There's a tv show on about it here right now, and I could totally see it working."

I flinched internally. I knew exactly which show she was referring to: an ex-CIA officer who had been burned and started picking up investigation cases on the side, using his finely-honed skillset. "P, it's not that easy."

"Nothing ever is, but it's a thought."

"Yeah. But..."

Parker's eyes went over my shoulder, and I could tell she was turning over possibilities and complications in that whip-smart brain of hers. "V, listen to me," she said finally. "You yourself just admitted you have an eight-year hole in your resume. Working for yourself is almost your only option at this point."

I couldn't argue with that. "Yeah?"

"So do what you can, and use what you have. Watching you work yesterday was mind-blowing. You can't throw away an entire career of experience."

"I'm not thrilled about it either, trust me. But..." I shrugged.

"And here you're supposed to be the smart one," she teased. "Since all three of us need gainful employment, I vote that we open our own detective agency. You're the brains, I'm obviously the beauty, and Gran is our hired muscle."

We both laughed at that, and I felt a little of the stress that had been pinching my shoulders ease. I'd done the right thing by coming home, by letting Parker put me back together. "That *does* sound like a television show. Or maybe we should aim higher, for Hollywood."

"I'll ask Gran to write our pitch letter tonight, then." Her smile grew wider. "Honestly, though, that would be incredible. We could offer tiers of services...all

11

the way from finding out if your man is cheating on you, to actually tossing his stuff in a dumpster. We're a full-service team."

"Yes to the first part, but the second part could get us arrested."

"Hmm, forgive me if I'm not feeling too guilty about that. God, how could I have been so blind for so long?"

I leaned across the table and squeezed her hand. "Maybe it was a recent thing. Why would he have stayed with you for so long otherwise?"

"You knew from the start, though."

I knew I had to choose my words carefully. "P, I didn't like him *personally*. Plenty of people don't get along on a personal level. I didn't know that he would have done this. There's no way I would have kept something like that from you."

"Yeah, I know. I'm sorry. I didn't mean that you knew all along…I just don't know how I couldn't have picked up on it sooner."

"You *did*," I reminded her. "I could pull up the exact date and time of the Skype logs when you implied *something* was off. You loved him. That makes it easy to assume you're just going through a rough patch."

"Don't let me do that ever again, okay? If your douchebag detector goes off on anyone I bring home ever again, let me know."

"That's an easy promise to make." I leaned back in my chair and sighed. "So word on the street is that you need a roommate. Can I skip the application process and just move right in?"

"Well, I don't know..." Parker twirled the pink-tipped ends of her blond ponytail around her finger. "You're not bringing any kitchen appliances, electronics, or hot single brothers to this relationship, I'll have to think it over. Duh, dumbass, of course you're moving in with me."

After lunch, Parker drove us to Magnolia Cemetery, where both Matthew and Sarah Chase were buried. She put the car in park, and we sat in silence for a moment before I took a deep breath and broke it.

"P...I'm so sorry."

"Don't be," she said softly. "You being here wouldn't have prevented it. And she was so proud of you...she had your 'service record' memorized down to the tiniest detail, and she bragged about it all the time. She told you to 'keep your butt on base,' remember?"

"How could I forget that conversation?" I tried to make my words light, but my fingernails were digging into my jean-clad thighs. P and I were both orphans now...although she had the comfort of knowing where her parents were buried, and I didn't know if mine were alive or dead and didn't really care. "Thank God for Gran."

"Amen to that. You okay?"

13

I forced myself to unclench my fingers. "Yes."

She did the best thing she could have, which was to open her door and get out, giving me a chance to pull myself together. I was in worse shape than I thought.

Come on Carmichael, things are always going to be harder before they get easier. Pull it together.

I took a deep breath and opened my door, stepping out into the hot Charleston sunshine. Cicadas buzzed in the trees as I followed Parker along the path that we were both all too familiar with, weaving around headstones until we reached a pretty area that overlooked the lagoon. Sarah had taken a lot of comfort from the location when Parker and I went with her, visiting the final resting place of the man who'd been ripped out of our lives way too soon.

It had been long enough that the grass around Sarah's headstone matched that of her husband's, the only thing that gave away the twenty years between the burials was the headstones. Matthew's was still in wonderful condition, of course, but you could tell it had been there longer, exposed to the elements, for far longer than his wife's.

Parker and I both knelt and, as one, split the bouquets we'd each bought from a street vendor outside the seafood restaurant. Half for both graves, one mixed bouquet for each of them. Parker looked lost in thought and I was too.

After a moment, I reached out and ran my fingers

14

over the engraved letters. Parker had opted for a headstone that matched her father's in style and content, although I could imagine that Sarah had had a say in it before she passed. Having your husband die seven years into your marriage probably gave you a more realistic sense of mortality.

"V?"

"Hmm?" I jerked myself away from my morbid thoughts.

"I was thinking about it on the way over here, and...I'm not really sure that I want to stay here."

I blinked, confused, not sure if she was referring to the cemetery or something else. "Stay where, specifically?"

"Charleston." Parker made a tiny adjustment to the flowers on her mother's grave before sitting back. "I've been thinking about this a lot, actually. I was going to talk to you about it the next time we had time to...I tried to talk about it with Shane but that obviously doesn't matter anymore."

I felt another stab of guilt. "Okay."

"I can't even drive within a few blocks of where my dad died. I just can't, I've never been able to. And now with my mom gone...there's not really anything to keep me here, you know? I mean, aside from Gran, obviously. But this city doesn't have a hold on me anymore. And I don't really think I can move on until I reset myself, start somewhere new. It's not like I have anything planned, but..." she let out her breath in a long sigh. "I think all this shit with Shane was the kick in the ass that I needed. Everything here reflects the past. I need to move on, but I don't think I can as long as I'm here. Does that make sense?"

More than she knew. "Yes. Do you know where you want to go?"

"No. All this happened in the past few days, and all I know is that I don't want to have to avoid the street where my dad died for the rest of my life. I don't want to worry that I'll cross paths with Shane. This town is way too small, so it's bound to happen."

I couldn't argue with that.

"I don't know, I just can't stay here if I want to get over everything, you know? It'll always be here if I want to come back and visit but..." Parker pulled her knees up to her chest and wrapped her arms around them, resting her cheek on skin that had bruises from leading her self-defense night classes. "Everything is coming together at the same time. I'm losing my job. Gran is being evicted from her florist shop. You're home for good. I think you were right that it's a sign. At the same time, though, I can't imagine leaving you or Gran behind. So I guess I'm just being selfish...or it's wishful thinking."

"You're assuming neither of us would want to go with you."

She swallowed hard. "You want to start over

16

somewhere else?"

"I have as much tying me here as you do. Nothing, except Gran. As long as you don't want to leave the country for a while, I'm game to go with you."

"I guess we just need to decide where we're going, then?"

I thought back over the last eight years of my life, all the places I'd visited or passed through. "If there's one thing my job taught me, it's that sometimes it'll land in your lap. Tomorrow let's sit down and start making it reality."

She nodded, then twisted her wrist to check her watch. "Shoot, we'd better get going if we want to hit the mall for you before we head over to Gran's."

I fussed over the flowers on Sarah's grave one last time, mentally thanking the woman who'd been more of a mother to me than my own biological one. Parker was right; her parents weren't here any longer, and I didn't want to run into mine by accident either. We'd both grown up here, but living overseas during my most formative adult years had cut all the ties that would have held me to Charleston.

Moving on would be the best way to start my life over, and I could only imagine doing it with my best friend by my side.

Gran still lived in the same house that her husband

had brought her to as a newlywed, and it was more familiar to me than my own childhood home. Bougainvillea spilled over the garden walls, but it was trimmed back to showcase the riot of other gorgeous flowers that could be seen both in and outside of the house. Gran's talent with flowers was an artless elegant thing, one that had landed her in the pages of *Southern Living* and *Better Homes and Gardens*. It was a gift that both Sarah and Parker had inherited.

Me, on the other hand? I could wilt a flower by just looking at it the wrong way, like a vampire. All of the plants I'd left behind in my Bulgarian apartment had been fake, to my landlady's despair.

In the lazy comfort of Gran's backyard, stuffed full of her amazing cooking, listening to her sweet drawl chirp away as she caught me up on all the latest news, I was more relaxed than I'd been in a very long time. I was slightly drowsy from the two glasses of wine I'd allowed myself, and the drone of the cicadas had faded in the twilight. Despite my resolve to move on wherever Parker wanted us to go, I'd miss the South. It was home to more wonderful memories with the Chase family than bad ones with my own, and I'd never fully acclimated to the winters of Russia and Bulgaria, or even the chilly dampness of Scotland. In Gran's backyard, the eight years away melted slightly and blurred around the edges.

I guess it was true that you could take the girl out

of the South, but you could never take the South out of the girl.

When Gran switched the topic to her flower shop and its impending closure, I forced myself to pay closer attention.

"And oh, I'm just not sure what to do. I'm no spring chicken, and most people would tell me that it's a sign that I should retire and enjoy myself." Gran sighed. "But I don't want to retire. I love what I do. I've had a few attorneys approach me offering to rent space in these new developments, but I..."

Parker sat up abruptly in her chair. "Gran, you didn't..."

"Well of course not, sweetpea, I can smell a rat from a mile away and they were all rats. Imagine Black-Eyed Susans squeezed in between a pizza chain and a cell phone store." She shuddered, and I knew exactly what she meant. Her shop was a downtown fixture, surrounded by other small shops like it, and she had to be one of the few flower shops in the area that did a brisk walk-in impulse purchase trade. Her magnolia corsages were especially popular with tourists, and Charleston's old money families didn't even consider ordering from anyone else. She'd already mentioned that she'd had multiple offers from them to fund her shop opening in another location, but Gran was as proud as they came. She might only be ten cents short of being able to purchase her own new building outright, but that was all it would take.

I exchanged a quick glance with Parker, and a corner of her mouth curled up before she leaned toward her grandmother. "Gran, would you be willing to reopen somewhere else if Vivian and I went in with you on it? She and I both are both going to be unemployed, and we agree it would be better to meet it head on."

"Hmm, what did you have in mind?" Gran's question was cautious, but I knew that she trusted both of us implicitly.

"With you in charge of the flowers, it would be a complete success. I've helped you out for years and Vivian..."

"I'll be the delivery driver," I inserted quickly, and all three of us laughed ruefully.

"Oh Vivian, I'm sure there's a green thumb inside of you somewhere, we just have to find it!"

"It's been in hiding for almost thirty years," I replied wryly. "I think delivery driver is a much safer choice when it comes to risk assessment."

"Well of course I'd rather go into business with you two than some slumlord rat...but where were you thinking? We can't afford any of the storefronts downtown on our own now, real estate being what it is."

"We were thinking about looking outside of Charleston," Parker offered carefully. Gran had lived her entire life in Charleston, and had seventy-six years of reasons to want to stay. "Both V and I agree that starting over fresh would be better for both of us."

Gran's gaze swung over to me just before she tucked her chin down, bright blue eyes sharp. "Hmm…I can see that, dearie."

"But we understand if you wouldn't want to leave," I started, only to have Gran wave her napkin at me.

"Vivian Carmichael, you two girls are the only family I have left in this world. If you think I'm going to let you take off and leave me here, then you've both got another think coming. Family is what really matters, not shops or houses or this dreadful bridge club I keep forcing myself to go to. No, I think if you two are going to start off on an adventure of your own, then I'd better go along with you."

Things happened faster than any of us had dared to believe was possible. While Parker and Gran focused on selling everything from Black-Eyed Susan's that could raise capital, I dove into online searches and analytics, looking for a place where we knew we could replicate the success Gran had had in Charleston. It was in an online social network group for florists where I found exactly what I was looking for: a shop that was going out of business due to inept management rather than lack of demand. It had been the pet project for a group of bored housewives only two hours away, in downtown Savannah, a business that gave them a reason to get together and have champagne socials once a week rather than focus on any actual increase in income. There weren't any real competitors nearby, and it was being sold with all the expensive equipment they'd dumped into it.

It really was fate. The trophy wives were moving on to form their own yogilates studio, and were only too happy to offload what they'd so quickly grown bored with. Two and a half weeks into our search, the three of us drove to Savannah to sign the closing paperwork, speeding to our new property after Gran handed over a hefty check that all three of us had contributed to.

"I'm in love," Parker sang, throwing her head back and twirling around in the empty shop.

"It really is gorgeous," I admitted. The front windows were enormous, just begging for displays of Gran and Parker's work, and the off-white walls and hardwood floor gave the entire shop an incredibly stylish yet mellow down-home feel.

"Joseph brought me here for our honeymoon," Gran sighed happily. "I always did have a soft spot in my heart for coastal Georgia. Now, Parker, you show me how to use this fancy camera so I can take pictures and start planning where everything will go."

Their voices faded behind me as I wandered into the back room. A cute little bathroom, functional office, tons of storage, and...a gigantic gun safe? Interesting...I'd read over the paperwork in excruciating detail, and I didn't remember that little detail being mentioned.

"Gran?"

"Yes sweetpea?" She bustled in behind me. "Oh how perfect, a nice wide door, probably right out onto the loading dock. Now I've got the keys for both the delivery vans they left, so we can move them over to that nice attorney's office for now."

"Uh-huh. P, do you have the pictures they sent us?"

"Yeah, I tucked them in with all the other paperwork. Why, what's up?"

I pointed at the metal behemoth hulking in the corner. "Do you remember anything about them leaving an arsenal?"

"Definitely not." Parker cocked her head curiously. "Where the hell do you think *that* came from?"

"Oh, I just bet one of those floozies hid her husband's guns in there," Gran fretted. "He didn't want to get rid of them, so she probably stashed them here."

Snickering a little at the idea of any of the trophy wife florists stashing a loaded gun safe in the back of their flower shop, I examined it carefully. "Maybe we're not giving them enough credit. Maybe they were money launderers. There could be piles of dirty money in here."

"Well we own it now, lock, stock and barrel." Parker peeked over my shoulder as I tried the solid handle.

It turned easily in my hand, and I swung the door open.

"Sorry to disappoint, ladies, but it's empty. No cash, no guns. I think Gran's guess is probably closest...they wanted to get rid of it because it didn't match the drapes, so they viewed their shop as a dumpster. I wonder what else we'll run across in this place?"

"Vivian, do you think we can sell it?"

"If we can get the combination, sure." I peered around the interior thoughtfully, then pointed at the numbers scrawled on a sticker pasted to the inside wall. "*Voilà*. I wonder if we should keep it, though."

"What in the world for?"

I shrugged, already assessing what size and type of shop-defense weapon we could keep in the safe. "We won't have to rent a safe-deposit box at the bank if we keep it. Hell, it's practically big enough to be a panic room if we get robbed."

"If you think so," Gran murmured. "Maybe we ought to think about buying a shotgun, then."

I don't know which one of us was more stunned, me or Parker.

"What? I'm no fool, I know that any no-good within spitting distance of this place would view us as an easy target to knock over. Who would suspect the sweet little lady behind the register was actually packing heat?"

"Oh my God," Parker choked. "First of all, Vivian would take out anyone stupid enough to mess with her..."

"Well, I was referring to myself, sweetpea. Now that I think about it, we ought to look at getting a security system installed. With a panic button under the front counter. I won't always have the two of you around to toss out any low-lifes that try to start something with me." She nodded briskly. "Oh, look at that office! I'll have that set up in no time. We'll move the desk against the other wall, though, and..."

Gran started snapping pictures of her soon-to-be dream office, and Parker and I exchanged incredulous looks before she shook her head and jotted down *security system* on the list she'd started. "I really need to stop underestimating her."

"You and me both. I agree with her, though...a security system would be a good idea. Shops that do a lot of cash business *are* viewed as quick and easy targets. I'd feel better about her being here alone from time to time if we knew there was a panic button and a security camera or two. Or three."

"Hey, that's your area of expertise, so you're the boss there. Do you think she was serious about the shotgun?"

"Yes, and I agree with that too."

Parker nodded; she and I both had been taught how to safely handle guns when we were in high school. Then all of the advanced training I'd received at the hands of the U.S. Government, of course. I was about to head out back to check out the vans when Parker let out a loud snort of laughter.

"What?"

"Oh, I totally just thought of the name for the shop," she snickered. "It just named itself."

"What's that?" I asked, echoed by Gran, who had wandered back over to us.

"Pistils. Get it? Three pistol-packing ladies playing with their stamens and...pistils."

Gran got it faster than I did, naturally, then she started chuckling too. "Oh Parker...you've always had a way with words. That's just perfect!"

Parker shook her head, still laughing. "No Gran, I'm totally kidding. It'll be Black-Eyed Susans, just like your old shop."

"This isn't my old shop," Gran said firmly, trying and failing to cover her smile. "This is our new shop...and I think Pistils will do just fine."

Chapter Two

"If we ever do this again," Parker groaned, dropping the last box onto one of the stacks surrounding us, "We are hiring movers. Preferably hot ones, so we can ogle them and drink wine while *they* do the hard work."

I laughed breathlessly, carefully setting down the box of glassware I'd carried in. "Agreed. But just think of how much money we saved."

"Stop ruining my hot sweaty mover fantasy with your practical words, Vivian Carmichael." She put her hands to the small of her back and stretched. "Ooooh, we're going to feel this tomorrow."

Relocating *and* starting a new business was expensive, so we'd decided to move ourselves and Gran instead of paying the insane price we'd been quoted for professional help. It had taken a week to pack up everything in Parker's apartment and Gran's little house, including the small amount of my own personal items that I'd left in Gran's spare room. Loading and the drive had been the easy part, unloading was not. Gran had fretted about us working too hard until we banished her to the shop with instructions to start calling in supplies. We were planning to open for business in two weeks, as long as all our licensure and tax information was squared away in time.

"And we still have to unpack," I said ruefully.

"Let's go rent a room in a hotel for the night. Preferably one with a jacuzzi."

Parker's eyes brightened. "Yeah?"

"I'd totally be down for it, but I have a feeling that Gran would somehow know, and we'd come back here in the morning to find she spent all night unpacking and putting everything away for us."

She groaned. "You're so right, she would. Well let's go turn the truck in, I'll follow you and we can pick up Gran and grab something for dinner on the way back. Chinese?"

"Always."

"Did they have Chinese restaurants in Sofia?"

"Yeah, and it wasn't half-bad, believe it or not. My landlady was always making home-cooked meals for me, though, so I didn't have to resort to takeout terribly often."

"Is Bulgarian food good?" I could tell she was curious, any time I offered up any information about my life there, she zeroed in on the details.

"It's delicious." I tossed her the keys she'd been looking for. "Let's hit the road."

Five hours later, we lay sprawled on our new couch in our new apartment, still surrounded by unpacked boxes. We'd eaten our takeout dinner at Gran's new cottage and then made her promise repeatedly that she wouldn't try to unpack anything remotely heavy without us there. We'd set up her bed, put the boxes of essential items in spots where she wouldn't have to bend or lift to get at the contents, and then dragged our sorry carcasses home.

It said a lot about my level of exhaustion that I didn't turn down the vodka shot that Parker handed me. "To success in starting over at life," she offered, clinking her glass against mine.

"I'll drink to that," I replied tiredly, before bolting the shot. She held up the bottle with her eyebrows raised and I shook my head. "We really are starting over."

"Gran is totally lapping us," she chuckled, pouring herself another shot. We'd arrived at Pistils to discover Gran hadn't just put in our first supply orders, she'd also reached out to our first customers: friends and family of the Charleston population that had been so sad to see her go. She'd already booked us two weddings and multiple pre-orders for birthdays and anniversaries. We'd also gained almost a thousand Facebook followers in one day. It was insane.

"Yeah she is. I guess we won't have to worry about whether or not the shop is going to be a success. I heard her say something about calling the newspaper social page editor too. Those Richie Riches love our Gran."

I smiled. Gran was definitely a sharp businesswoman, but she had a heart of gold too. We both knew that any child who had entered Black-Eyed Susan's left clutching a free flower or two, and Gran had always made corsages and boutonnieres come prom-time for any high-schooler that couldn't afford them. All they had to do was come into the shop and ask, and she'd tell them to come back day-of, no proof of income needed. It was a trait that she'd definitely passed on to her daughter and granddaughter.

"I vote that we call it quits for the night. We can unpack and then start looking for jobs tomorrow." Both Parker and I had agreed that Gran should be Pistils' only full-time employee until we had a better idea of what business would be like. The outlook was considerably better than just twenty-four hours before, but we didn't want to chance it.

Plus, being financially conservative gave us an excuse to share an apartment. It was common sense as we knew one of us would always be at the other's place anyway, and Parker had found us a deal we couldn't pass on: our new apartment was close to Pistils, close to Gran, and came with appliances plus the utilities included in the rent. After I ran my own background check on the owner and looked for any speck of shadiness connected to the complex, we'd rented our new home.

Parker hummed an agreement to my words, then tugged her hair out of its disheveled ponytail. "Have you thought any more about what you want to do?"

"I've got some ideas rolling around in my head." I don't know why I bothered to fib, she saw right through me.

"Want some suggestions?"

"Sure."

"Well, let me tell you some of what you're good at...I would suggest bodyguard, language tutor, or travel guide."

I shuddered. "Cross that last one off, too many bad memories."

"Hacker for hire is still an option."

"No, definitely not. I'm not as good as you think I am."

"I *saw* how good you are, don't be modest."

"I'm not. What you saw me do is just scratching the surface of what a real hacker can do...if I'd followed a different career track while I was there, that would be one thing. I was more of a HUMINT type."

"What the heck is that?"

"Gathering information from actual people, you know, one-on-one. As opposed to gathering it with technology. So essentially I got basic training, like Hacker 101, but nothing advanced." Ah, memories.

She shrugged. "It's not like people would be hiring you to hack into the Pentagon...or at least, I hope not. You could handle stuff like you did for me...getting into a cheating boyfriend's email."

"Although I would have no problem doing it, some of what I'd probably be asked to do is illegal. I don't want you to have to shake down Gran for bail money for me."

"Bail bondsman? As employment, not to get you out of jail. Repo-woman?"

"Parker, you're killing me," I groaned. "I do not want to be a repo-woman."

"But you'd be so *good* at it! Even when we were kids, you just had a sixth sense about things. You knew where to go and what to do...you always found the most eggs at Gran and Papa's Easter egg hunt."

"Can I put that on my resume?"

She let out an exasperated huff. "Hey, whatever floats your boat. What do you *want* to do?"

"Honestly? To get some cash right off the bat, I'll probably do some language tutoring. While I keep looking for a job with health insurance."

"How many languages do you speak now?"

"Fluently or passably?"

"Umm, enough to get us around another country on vacation."

"Eight."

"*What?*"

I laughed. "I included English on that list. Fluently, five. I can curse like a sailor in the other three if that counts, and I could definitely get us around those countries on vacation."

"Jesus, V, what do they put in the water up there at MIT?"

"Caffeine."

She shook her head slowly. "I wouldn't be surprised."

"Parker, *ya vtomyvsya.*"

"Did you just curse me out?"

I chuckled again and started to stand. "It means 'I'm tired' in Ukrainian."

"Uh-huh, I knew it. No caffeine in the water, Carmichael stalls out." Parker slowly stood too, then reached over to give me a tight hug. "Hey, if you ever want to want to talk about when you learned Ukrainian, I promise not to tell anyone."

"I know you wouldn't." I squeezed her back. "I'm just not ready to yet. Someday. Just not yet."

"All right roomie, I'll see you in the morning. Good night."

"Good night." Bed and sleep had never seemed so incredibly seductive. All our new furniture had been delivered that morning under the apartment manager's watchful eye, but I realized with a silent groan that I still had to make the bed. Gran had been in charge of packing our individual boxes of Day One Necessities and Essentials, or DONE, as Parker had rightly predicted we'd be. So luckily for me, I wouldn't have to dig around for pajamas or toothpaste, but those freshly laundered sheets wouldn't jump on the bed by themselves.

I gave Parker another hug as we parted ways at her

bedroom door, only steps from my own. They couldn't have looked more different; Parker's was packed full of boxes, bags and personal items, belongings kept from childhood right up through her recent split with Shane. Mine had exactly eight boxes, including the DONE care package. I stood eyeing the room, thinking that it really resembled an Army barracks, except that I'd caved to Parker and ordered a queen-sized bed instead of...

"Have you got room in your bed for two?"

"Your bed in Sofia is barely big enough for one, and we made that work."

I flinched against the doorframe as though the memory had been a bullet. I wasn't ready to think too much about David, not yet. I'd kept myself too busy to think, busy enough to ward off the lists of regrets; I'd never mentioned him again to Parker. But now it felt as though I'd left him there by the Potomac only seconds ago, still with enough time to turn around and agree to what I knew we both wanted more than anything.

And I'd be a liar if I said there weren't moments I'd regretted not turning back around. Those were the bad nights, when I muffled the sobs that I didn't want Parker to hear. God, I missed him so much.

Tears were trying to work their way up, but I forced them back down. I'd become something of an expert at controlling my tear ducts, I could switch them on and off like light bulbs...but only when there weren't real emotions involved.

And tonight, the switch apparently wasn't working right. It had to be the vodka. *Jesus, pull yourself together.*

The burner phone was a bump in my back pocket. I knew Parker had seen it, just as I'd noticed her look of surprise when I suggested we duck into the cell phone store at the mall where I'd dropped almost a grand on a brand-new high-tech smartphone right after I got back. But she didn't ask questions, because she knew that I'd tell her when I was ready...if I ever was.

I took a deep breath and stood straight, then crossed the room, digging into the DONE box and making my bed with clinical efficiency. I could hear Parker still rummaging around behind her closed door, so I took a quick shower before heading back into my new room, killing the light on the way in. Gran had gifted me with a bedside table from her spare room, and I set the phone on top of it after checking the battery status. *"Keep it on, all the time."*

I considered and then rejected the idea of pajamas, instead climbing under the sheets nude before burying my face in the pillow, forcing my eyes to shut.

Okay Carmichael, there you go. You've made your bed, haven't you? Now lie in it.

Chapter Three

Pistils was, in no uncertain terms, an overnight hit in Savannah. One month after we officially opened, business was brisk enough to budget in both myself and Parker a part-time salary. Not only had Gran's social contracts bloomed into smashing success, but the trophy wife former owners I'd been so quick to dismiss turned out to be more valuable to us than anything else. It may have been due to nostalgia initially, but after an order or two, those women validated us in Savannah. They didn't just patronize Pistils themselves, they actively starting referring business our way in addition to the thrice-weekly standing order they had for a gigantic arrangement to grace the front desk of their new yogilates studio. They got so many questions about the flowers that they finally gave up and asked Gran for a stack of business cards to sit discreetly next to the vase.

They were all gone within two days.

Gran was in her element. She was working with flowers, the thing she loved best in the world after Parker and me. She charmed the men who came in or called to order for their wives, girlfriends and mistresses, inevitably up-selling them on orders with her sweet voice. Women loved her because she'd be honest, but kind...*Now I love that flower too, but dearie, I think that yellow just* wouldn't *do justice to that* gorgeous *skin of yours, not to mention that* hair! And just as in Charleston, she was handing out free flowers to kids left and right.

It was enough to make the accountant we'd contracted sheepishly admit that he would suspect us of cooking the books if his wife *and* sister hadn't already mentioned seeing one of Gran's arrangements while out on the town somewhere. My offhand comment about stashing cash in the inherited gun safe came to fruition as we started keeping petty cash in there, right next to the old Mossberg shotgun I'd picked up at a flea market. I'd cleaned and tested it repeatedly myself before taking Gran and Parker to the range to make sure they were comfortable with it there.

Parker was in seventh heaven too. She'd picked up an afternoon job at a mental-health clinic, and when she wasn't there, she was at the shop, putting flowers together in a way that I'd never think of myself, but always sold out immediately. I did my part where I knew it would be best utilized: writing out the cards to accompany the orders that streamed in via phone, website and our new app, making deliveries, calling in supply orders, cleaning and locking up the shop every night. It might have driven other people crazy, but I welcomed the repetitive tasks, because it kept the stress and eventual anxiety at bay.

I'd also picked up some language tutoring jobs that paid quite well thanks to Gran (*Well isn't he clever! Russian too? You know, our Vivian speaks Russian fluently and is tutoring students on a limited number of...why yes! I can schedule something right here from the shop!*), and I was grateful for it, but the peace I'd bought myself was starting to wear thin.

The burner phone never rang, and I didn't know whether I wanted it to or not.

And this was not what I wanted to do with my life.

I wasn't ashamed or resentful. Until the day I died, I'd owe Gran and Parker for finding enough work around Pistils to allow me to justify drawing a paycheck. But the itch that had been triggered under my skin, in a hotel room in Cambridge so many years ago, had only receded a little bit while my soul licked its wounds and started to heal. I'd found what I was *meant* to do while working for the CIA, and even as I cringed to think about it, I knew that it was also what I really *wanted* to do.

Not for all the money in the world would I have ever gone back to them, but the *hunt*, the slow and methodical cultivation...now I could understand why some people loved building ships in a bottle.

That was me...I needed that delicate dance between partners, the build-up, the goal...knowing that if I did my job correctly, it would result in the most satisfying of outcomes...a ship in a bottle.

A mobster in prison.

Ships in bottles, mobsters in prison...are they really that different? One good smash and there's going to be hell to pay, not to mention a big mess.

In addition to my restlessness, I'd developed a heightened sense of paranoia. I'd be a fool to think that the CIA wasn't keeping tabs on me in some fashion, even if it was assigning rookie officers to track my movements, or passing it off to the FBI. I resented it, but more for Gran and Parker than for me...the first time Parker introduced me to a really cute guy that she'd met, my immediate thought snapped to the realization that his name and personal information were probably being dutifully logged somewhere, and it was all because of me.

And every single day, I thought about David.

Gran and Parker weren't stupid, they could see that I wasn't happy. After the initial bloom fell from the rose, so to speak, Gran started fretting over me more. Parker would start to ask me something and then bite her tongue. I didn't know what to tell them or even what to say. Maybe *I* was that ship in a bottle, except that I wanted to violently rebel against the glass around me. My guilt over making them worry only made things worse.

We'd been in business for seven months and fourteen days when the seas got stormy...but not in a bad way. Sometimes ships need a rogue wave to smash them out of the bottle.

It was an unexpectedly busy afternoon...one of Savannah's city council members had passed away, and we had condolence bouquet orders pouring in. We'd flipped the sign to Closed, but as we had a few pick-up orders for the afternoon, we didn't lock the door. I was filling out the millionth condolence note when she tripped through the door. Mrs. Rockingham.

Or as I preferred to think of her, Patient Zero.

She'd barely cleared the entrance before she burst into tears, and Parker and I exchanged glances. She'd proven repeatedly to be the best one to deal with emotional types. I was excellent at superficial customer service, but I had little patience for anyone who went to pieces in front of others like that. It probably said a lot about my state of mind at that moment.

"Something red, blood red," Mrs. Rockingham...Trish, as she'd told us to call her, sniffled. "That *bitch*! I want him to know that I know!"

"All right then," Gran soothed. "What's the...ah, occasion?"

Trish wiped at her nose and Parker handed her a tissue. "I've thought for a long time now that my husband was having an affair. For about the past four months, maybe? You just don't want to...you know? I didn't want to think it was possible! We have three children! But the housekeeper found a pair of panties in one of our guest rooms, and I..." She burst into full-on tears.

Despite our busy afternoon, the walk-in traffic had been surprisingly light. At Gran's subtle gesture, I eased over and locked the front door. It was a thoughtful tactic, to keep anyone from walking in off the street and seeing one of Savannah's most famous society-wives crying her eyes out about the man that did her wrong. Gran stroked her shoulder.

"Oh, we've all been there at some point, dearie. Why don't you take a seat here on this stool and tell us what happened? Let it all out, you'll feel better."

Trish was only too happy to oblige. Details that she'd die before admitting to her socialite friends boiled up...his unexplainable irritation, his repeated absences and late nights at work, the faint puff of another woman's perfume when she leaned in for a kiss.

"But I'm afraid I'm going to look like a psycho!" she finally wailed.

"Oh honey, why? Based on what you told us, no one would blame you!"

"The court won't take any of that into account," she replied bitterly. "Our pre-nup specified 'proof or admission of infidelity' and none of what I just told you is proof! I quit my job for him! He said that I would never have to worry about any of those things, that he wanted me to stay home and take care of our kids if that's what made me happy. And look where that got me!"

"Oh honey...I'm so sorry. You don't have any hard evidence?"

"No, none. What am I supposed to do, go in front

of the judge and claim women's intuition? I'd look like a freak!"

"Have you thought about having someone, ah, get hard evidence?" Parker asked carefully.

"Well I...yes! But what am I supposed to do? Call one of those people that advertise during trashy afternoon television? They'd probably run right to him and...no. I'd rather die of shame than have my family's name dragged through the mud like that. I just...I don't know what to do!" Here she broke into a fresh round of wailing.

Parker and Gran exchanged glances over the woman's heaving shoulders.

"I...well, I apologize if I'm being indelicate, but I have a suggestion," Gran said slowly. "I know someone that can get that 'hard evidence' for you, if there is any. She is extremely discreet. No one will need to know until you're nailing that cheating bastard to the wall in court."

All of my *oh-shit* detectors went off right then and there, but Parker was already falling into line, and she nodded to Gran, who immediately bent back over the woman's shoulders. "Would you like us to have her call you?"

"Are you...is she...I just can't afford to have this get out! Maybe it would be better if I just..."

"Oh dearie, don't you worry about that a bit. She'll find out, and she'll give you the honest truth, whether you want to hear it or not. Because you're tearing yourself to pieces thinking about it, and that's not good for you or your beautiful babies."

She nodded slowly. "I know, you're right. I'm so sorry, bursting in on you like this, please just forget I said anything."

"Now forgive *me* for being rather bald about this, but do you really think that's the best thing to do? If he's acting the way you described, you already know that something isn't right."

Her face started to crumple again. "I know. I just can't afford to let this get out."

"Well then let me suggest this...why don't I ask her to look into it? If she doesn't find anything, then that's the end of it. If she does...well, she can give you that information and you can do what you want with it."

Trish's shoulders sagged. "Please...I can't tell you enough that I can't afford to have this get out. If he or anyone else found out, he'd bury me before I even had a chance to find a lawyer to take my case."

"In my experience, lawyers will take a case if you hand them a signed check for their retainer." Gran gave her shoulders another pat. "Why don't you give us a call or, better yet, come on back into the shop in a week. At least you'll know one way or the other by then."

She dabbed at her nose with the sodden tissue. "Well, all right. Just please, remember that this can't..."

"It can't get out. Oh honey, I know, I know. You

go on home now and let us take care of this."

It took several more pats and hugs and reassurances before Trish was on her way out the door. I leaned against the wall behind the counter, silently watching as Parker locked the door behind her. Gran was the one who came over to face me, her expression resolute.

"Vivian…"

"No."

"Young lady, I'm not asking you, I'm telling you." I hadn't seen Gran this stern since she had caught Parker and me digging a swimming hole in the middle of her backyard when we were nine, and it brought me up short. "You need to get out of this shop right now, before you start resenting it and the place it has in your life. You may think you're restless now, just wait until a few more months have passed and you're still not happy with what you're doing. Now I may not know all of what you were doing for the army for the past eight years, but I know you weren't writing thank you cards and making flower deliveries. Get out there and do something other than that…get out of this shop and go do something that's worthy of how smart you are. You're not even tapping your potential, and right now we need our Vivian back and happy and *satisfied* again."

Gran finally stopped to take a breath, and I let my gaze slip over to Parker, stunned.

She was anxious, I could see that, but she took a

deep breath and nodded. "Vivian, how many times have I told you that taking care of us is what you *do*? You always have, and I don't see the harm in you going and doing something easy like this. You know how. I was in her position a few months ago, and you helped me without even thinking about it. This will be easy for you. And if she wants to pay you for it, all the better."

She was skipping along the razor's edge of saying too much, but when I turned back to Gran, she gave me a long look in return. For the first time, it made me wonder if Gran knew more about my supposed stint with the "army" than she'd ever let on. "Vivian, go. Get out of this shop before you wilt the flowers with that scowl, and help that poor woman. Just like you did Parker."

"You can't be serious right now."

"Oh, I'm serious, young lady. Now shoo. Parker will help me close up shop, and I don't want to see you back in here until you've found something out."

Looking to my best friend got me absolutely zero help, and I gave her my best *I'm going to kill you and I know how to hide the body* look. "Gran..."

"Out! And don't come back until you've brought us something to give her." Gran fluttered her delicate blue-veined hands at me.

This was a battle I wasn't going to win in the here and now. Less than a minute later, I was behind the wheel of my car, silently fuming. This wasn't what I wanted to do.

Wasn't it?

Yes, of course I did. Ferreting out hidden information was the whole reason I'd gone through interview after interview, polygraph tests and psychological examinations. Then it was why I'd given years of my life to the CIA. Even after I got past all the preconceived Hollywood notions about espionage, I'd found it all to easy to shed any moral qualms or reservations that case officers too often grappled with. As someone I loved once put it, there were good guys and bad guys, and I slipped past the guilt and the questions far too easily. Did that make me a sociopath? No...but it was probably what they'd concluded in my file just before it was filigreed with lies and buried.

They'd trained me to turn a blind eye to any shame or guilt over what I did to get to the truth. Why should I start succumbing to them now? It would have meant that Parker was still with Shane, and even that thought was enough to make rage poke back through the holes I thought I'd filled and buried.

Why should I give a damn about morality or legality? I'd drawn a paycheck for far too many years specifically for ignoring and even gutting both.

I sat far too long in my car behind the shop, long enough for Parker to come out and find me. I'd have to warn her that, in the future, yanking open a car door and plopping into a passenger seat was a good way to get kidnapped or killed.

Not by me, never in a million years by me. But just as she'd stated so firmly before, my thoughts always turned to taking care of her and Gran. They didn't need me to babysit them; Parker in particular was more than capable of defending herself and her grandmother if it came down to a physical fight. But I'd seen so much horror, so many devious tricks that could so easily go unanticipated, that they scrolled through my brain unbidden. There was ugliness and evil in the world that no one could prepare for unless you'd seen it firsthand for yourself, had it burned into your brain for the rest of your life.

"V, listen," Parker started after a moment. "Don't freak out on me, okay? We're just both so worried about you. Especially since we both know you'd die before you complained or asked for help. And we're not saying you need *help*," she hastened to say. "But you need to do something that will...I don't know...*challenge* you. And you're so far above what a normal job here can offer you, you've got to find something that will push you and make you think. You've been surviving the past few months by not thinking at all."

I sat, stunned into silence by her slicing through all the bullshit and identifying the real issue that kept me up at night, kept me still cauterizing feelings whenever

48

they tried to whisper to me in my weakest moments. The burner phone never rang, and it was only in recent weeks when I'd started allowing myself to wonder if it ever would. To wonder if I should let the battery run down just before I smashed the thing to pieces.

Just as I'd been trained to do. A burner phone was meant to be destroyed, to make any evidence of its existence splinter and drift into pieces that could never be put back together again. No trail, no links, no proof.

"And you can't do that...just please...do this. Do *something*. You've been numb ever since you got back, and we need *you* back, not the mask you keep putting on day after day. You're not going to scare me, so please just do whatever it is you would do in situations like this. Please. We need *you* back."

Her words tumbled around inside my mind, and I heard the truth in them. I just wasn't sure if it was a truth I wanted to validate. But if Gran had seen through the mirage I'd thought was bulletproof, then there was no point in trying to fool her granddaughter as well.

I started the car.

"People with something to hide get comfortable after a while," I said mechanically. "And comfort makes them careless. If he's cheating, that should be easy to find out. Maybe not tonight. But he'll blow it eventually. Probably sooner rather than later if it's been going on for a while."

Parker nodded silently, but I could see the gleam in her eyes.

"And the longer it's been going on, the more likely that he's been getting careless. Going to the same places, not bothering to make excuses. If his wife didn't demand answers after the first escapade or two, he's already assumed that she never will. Here, use my phone..." At a stoplight, I wriggled it out of my back pocket and handed it to her. "Do a web search for his name and then find out the names of his executive staff members."

"Okay..." Parker's fingers were already flying over the phone, following my instructions. "And then what?"

"Look for the most recent images of him with them."

"Men or women?"

"Both." I could feel the months' worth of anxiety and frustration slowly leaving me, like air leaving a balloon. Not with a sudden pop, but an easy slow leak. Just as Matthew Parker had shown us when Sarah had reluctantly retreated to their bedroom with a migraine following a particularly raucous childhood birthday party for Parker, only two weeks before he died. *We don't want to leave this mess for Mom to clean up, let's make sure it's all gone when she gets up tomorrow. Here, Vivi, put a piece of tape on the balloon before you try to pop it. You put the pin through the tape, it won't make a loud noise. It'll just leak out slow and quiet, then we can throw it away."*

That was my months of frustration, slowly leaking away as I gave Parker more tips to narrow down our search. And to her credit, she was the one who latched onto the photo.

"Whoa, look at this," she murmured as I slid to a stop at an intersection. I took a quick look at the grainy photo she'd found, immediately recognizing the subtle clues that gave away so much. Richard Rockingham at a company charity event from a few months before. Standing a fraction of an inch closer to a woman from the marketing department than would normally be comfortable. Her head thrown back with laughter that was belied only by the way the camera had caught her eyes coyly regarding him from their corners. A hand that had started to reach for her waist, the way she'd thrown her weight onto one foot so that her hip cocked in his direction.

"Well that was easy. If you can also find out if she's married, and what her husband's name is, that would be amazing."

Parker did it within five minutes.

"And now see if either of them have a social media account."

As I drove around town, I threw Parker challenge after challenge, and she'd meet them. Three hours later, we were parked in front of what we'd narrowed down to be

Mr. Rockingham's most likely location, based on cross-referencing everything from his company's list of charities they'd officially sponsored to my calling hotels and pretending to be Mr. Rockingham's personal assistant, attempting to validate recent charges to his company-issued credit card.

As we sat outside one of the many chain hotels that were clustered around I-526, Parker looked at me cautiously. "Did you have to do a lot of this?"

"I didn't, no, not specifically," I sighed, reaching over and squeezing her hand. More of the toxic anger had leaked out of me as each step we took narrowed down the vast array of possibilities facing us. "It's more a question of...human behavior. As much as we all think we're unique and clever, we're actually very predictable. Humans are painfully predictable, actually. I didn't...I had different reasons for tracing those patterns, but it's all the same in the end."

She nodded slowly. "That makes sense. Do you really think they're here?"

"Oh yeah." I gestured toward the cherry-red BMW parked just behind the silver Mercedes sedan, cars we'd identified from their public Facebook photos and Twitter accounts. "That's them all right. This place doesn't have conference rooms and it's not where their company puts up people from out of town. I can't think of any other reason that they'd be here."

"That makes sense, I get it. I'm just amazed at how you managed to link one thing to another like that."

"Human behavior," I repeated. "When you have a starting point, like we did, it's easy to follow him from Point A to Point Z. Mrs. Rockingham said that she'd been noticing how weird he'd been acting for the past four months. Plenty of time for him to get sloppy about covering his tracks."

"You're five steps ahead of him."

"Sometimes that's what keeps you alive." I reclined the seat back enough so that I was still able to see above the dashboard. "Now we wait. Ideally I'd have something better than my phone to get pictures with, but it'll do for now."

"We can afford a better camera," she murmured, but when I looked sharply in her direction, she was already reclining her seat too, pulling her own phone out.

Luck was on our side...I'd prepared myself to wait for hours, but either Mr. Rockingham and his girlfriend had a head start on us, or he just wasn't up for all-night sex marathons any longer. We'd only been parked there forty-five minutes when I spotted him walking cautiously out of a ground-level hotel room. He was wearing a suit, but it had that barely-rumpled look indicating that it may have been yanked off of him and discarded onto the floor or draped over a chair for a few hours. Everything was in place, but just very slightly off.

He'd barely taken five steps out of the room when a woman in a black dress followed, trying to wriggle back into a cheerful yellow jacket without dropping her purse. Her hair was a mess, and she swatted at the strands dangling around her face before calling out to Mr. Rockingham in a low voice. He swung around immediately, and she took the opportunity to wrap her arms around his neck, pulling him down for a kiss. It lasted only a few seconds before he stiffened and pulled away, hissing something at her. We couldn't hear what was said, but it was easy to imagine. His face was a mask of irritation and she flinched back immediately before recovering. She renewed her struggle with her blazer, finally making it in, and then tried running manicured nails through her knotted coiffure.

When she started to follow him again, Mr. Rockingham snapped something back at her, and this time she slammed to a stop, glowering slightly at his figure as he strode away. The alarm on his silver Mercedes chirped, and he threw himself behind the wheel, cranking the engine to life before he'd even yanked the door shut behind him. He took off, not slowing down as he sped away, apparently not even sparing a glance for his lover.

She stood staring after him, frustration, anger and surprise battling on her face. Mid-thirties, rich chestnut hair with highlights that were just barely obvious as a salon job, petite body lithe and trim. The old me would have wondered what the hell she saw in Mr. Rockingham, but I'd seen enough to know that it probably boiled down to money, power and attention.

"So…" Parker started slowly, "Do we say anything to her?" I could hear the tiny electronic shutter clicks from her phone as she snapped pictures along with me.

"Nope. She'd be on the phone with him in a heartbeat, freaking out so bad that he'd have a lawyer speed-dialed before we could count to ten. *She* is not our problem. You wanted us to solve a mystery, it's solved."

"V…" she started, but paused as the unknown brunette turned and stalked back into the hotel room. Without speaking, I switched over to video since I knew Parker was taking still pictures. Not that it mattered so much with a smartphone, but covering all our bases was imperative. Neither of us spoke for another five minutes, until she came striding back out, hair smoothed back into place, makeup repaired. She stopped to remove and throw her heels into the passenger seat before tossing her purse after them and then speeding off in the BMW.

"So predictable," I sighed, locking my phone before reaching down to move my seat back into an upright position. Parker followed suit.

"So did you do stuff like *that*?"

"Not exactly." My irritation and what I was slowly identifying as a sense of betrayal by Gran and Parker was slowly tapping away in the back of my mind again, letting itself be known. "I mean, if I needed a reason to find something to hold over someone, something to exploit, I could definitely do it. But I would have gone after his infidelity as a weakness, something to exploit."

Parker picked up on the edge in my voice immediately. "V, I'm sorry. I know we pretty much pushed you into doing this."

"You think?"

"But we only did it because we love you, and we're worried about you."

"You don't need to worry about me. I can take care of myself."

"You keep insisting that you will take care of me, and of Gran, and of yourself. What's wrong with letting us take care of you for once?"

I wanted to argue, but I knew I didn't have a leg to stand on. There wasn't anything, at that moment in time, that only I was qualified to protect us from. Maybe I needed to get over myself.

"P, listen. Thank you. I love you and Gran so very much for thinking that way. But you don't have to. I'm...I'll *be* fine. I promise."

"I know you wouldn't just accept that from me." Parker stared out through the front windshield. "So why don't you accept that if we know you better than anyone else in the word, that we might also know what's best for you?"

Her words were a loving slap in the face, and I sagged back into the seat without a reply.

"And neither of us need to know what happened," she continued doggedly, "To know how unhappy you are. Vivian, you left pieces of your heart back there, and I can't fill those. All I can do is make sure you know that we love you and we'd do anything for you. I can't replace those parts of you that belonged to David, or to your job, and I wouldn't even dream of trying. But as long as you choose to be *here*, I will never stop trying to take care of *you*."

A heart could beat without a brain, modern medicine had proved that. But a brain without a heart was a husk, a remnant waiting to to be crushed into dust. And I was terrified, deep down inside, that I was slowly fading away, turning into that husk. I didn't know that I was crying until I felt the teardrops hit the corners of my mouth. Parker took a deep breath.

"I'm sorry, V. I'm not saying all of this to hurt you. But you *are* hurting, and since you're my best friend...my *sister*, I'm not going to sit around being happy myself when you're so miserable."

"You can't force someone to be happy."

"I know. But any tiny little thing that Gran and I can do to push you back toward finding joy in some way, we are going to do. Are you telling me that you would have rather been tutoring that Beaumont brat in Russian than what we just spent the afternoon doing?"

I smiled despite myself. "God no."

"Did you enjoy what we did?"

A long moment passed before I answered her. "Yes, I did. It was a challenge, and I felt...I don't know...useful."

"You're going to give a very unhappy woman some answers. That's beyond useful."

The direction this conversation was going was dangerous, and I started the car to head back to Pistils. "I think, right now, we'd be a lot more useful back at work. Those flowers aren't going to deliver themselves."

I banished Mrs. Rockingham to the back of my mind, and was honestly surprised when she came back into the shop five minutes before closing time, exactly a week later. She was considerably more composed than when we'd seen her previously, and she looked around the shop cautiously before her gaze lighted on Gran. Pure relief washed over the careful mask that was her face.

"Ah, hello...I'm not sure if you remember me, but..."

"Why of course we do! And you're so thoughtful...we're just now closing up so we'll lock the door and sit down and have a nice chat."

She dropped gratefully onto the stool that Parker pushed her way. "Thank you. First, please let me apologize for my behavior the last time I was here. I was upset, but that was no excuse for barging in on you that way."

"Oh honey, if you *hadn't* been upset, I would have been even more concerned than I was."

"I know, but..." She twisted her fingers together nervously, and I noticed that her expensive-looking manicure was picked at on all ten fingers and her cuticles were red. "After I left here last week, and calmed down, I did a lot of thinking. At first I didn't plan to come back because, well, of course I was embarrassed about the way I'd behaved. And maybe I just needed to vent. But then I...well...I know a woman is supposed to look the other way..."

"Why?" Gran asked bluntly, and I was glad she'd beat me to it since it had been on the tip of my tongue.

"Exactly," Trish replied gratefully, before letting out a long sigh. "Our children are old enough to ask why Daddy is grumpy all the time, and why Mommy cries so much. Our oldest flat out asked the other day if we were going to get divorced...I guess a classmate's parents are going through one. And of course I said no at the time, but it made me do a lot of thinking. It's one thing for this to be affecting me, but when my *children* are picking up on it...that's where I draw the line. I won't stay with him if it's true."

Parker slipped into the back room, and I instinctively knew that she was going for the photos we'd taken, printed out, and stashed in the gun safe.

"And so I just thought I'd ask...I didn't want to call, I know you're busy...but did your, ah, investigator...?"

"She did," Gran soothed. "Would you like to know what she found out?"

Trish licked her lips, then sat up straighter on her stool. "Yes, please."

"Well then, I'll let her talk to you herself."

Surprised, I shot Gran a *WHAT?* look, and she gave me one right back that clearly said *Young lady, get your britches over here right now and help this poor woman.*

Ugh. Well, at least all the grooming I'd done for potential foreign assets would come in handy. It might be only superficial on my part, but I remembered how proud I'd been when I'd get another one to trust me, to open up and spill secrets of the most toxic variety. I put down the box of greeting cards I'd been unpacking and joined the three women at the counter.

"Mrs. Rockingham..."

"Trish, please."

"Trish, I do have some answers for you, but I need to ask you...what exactly do you want? Do you want me to just give you the pictures I was able to take? Or do you want me to tell you what I saw?"

She flinched at the word *pictures*, but swallowed hard and nodded. "Everything, please."

Parker handed me the sealed envelope she'd retrieved, and I looked the woman directly in the eyes. "Although I wasn't able to personally witness any actual acts of adultery taking place, I did witness and photograph your husband leaving a hotel room with Melanie Churchill, the manager of the marketing department at Rockingham Industries."

"Melanie?" Trish gasped, just before her brows came together and red flooded her face. "I can't...she and I were sorority sisters, and I actually recommended her for the job when...that *bitch*! Are you sure?"

I handed her the envelope and she tore into it, almost spilling the photos in her haste. She began flipping through them rapidly, stopping when she came to the one where Melanie got her goodbye kiss in. It was definitely the most damning of all the pictures we'd taken, and Trish's slowly-melting cool blew up right before our eyes.

"I knew it. I *knew* it. I knew that he was cheating, but with one of my *friends*...and how could she do this to me? I just saw her last week and we chatted for a good ten minutes about...*that fucking bitch*!"

I clamped my lips between my teeth to keep from smiling, as it would have been wholly inappropriate at that moment. "I'm sorry, Trish. I wish I'd had better news for you."

"Oh, no, this is exactly what I needed. I *knew* he was cheating, I just didn't have proof. These..." she waved the photos clenched in her hand, "Prove that I wasn't crazy or imagining things. If I didn't have these, he'd be gas...gassing..."

"Gaslighting," I supplied automatically.

"Yes, gaslighting. Calling me crazy is his go-to insult whenever we argue and...well, I won't burden you with that. Is there anything else I should know?"

I shook my head. "A photo of them kissing in front of a hotel is something his attorney won't be able to explain away very easily. May I offer some advice?"

"Yes, please!"

"If you don't already have this in place already, withdraw half of all the money you have in joint bank accounts and put it in one under only your name. If he catches wind of...well, some people are vindictive enough to drain the entire account and you'd be left high and dry. Then hire the best divorce attorney you can, and do it all in one day, don't give him a chance to catch on...you want to get the drop on him. Do you understand what I mean?"

She nodded gratefully. "Yes, yes, anything else?"

"Listen to whatever your divorce attorney tells you to do, he or she will know more than me. Do you have one in mind?"

"Yes...my sister went through an ugly divorce a few years back. Her husband...*ex*-husband, rather, was a very powerful lobbyist, and we were worried that she'd come away with nothing. Her attorney was marvelous, he got her the house, the cottage, alimony, child support..."

"Good," I said quickly. "I'd call him as soon as you leave here. Ask your sister if she has a direct cell phone number for him, so you don't have to wait until tomorrow."

"I will. Oh God...I can't believe I'm saying this, but I actually feel better. I might feel worse later, but right now I'm just...I feel like a ten-ton weight has been lifted off my shoulders." She slid off the stool and reached out for my hand. "Thank you, thank you so much. Please tell me how much I owe you for doing this."

I blinked, surprised. "Nothing. I didn't say that I would be charging you, I'm not going to come back at you with a bill now."

"Please, you have to accept something."

"Trish, I was able to do what I did based on experience in a previous career. I'm not a licensed private investigator."

"Well, I'm going to give you some unsolicited advice. You should really think about becoming one." She set her Chanel purse onto the counter and reached into the front pocket for a check. "What's your name?"

"Honestly, I can't..."

"It's Vivian Carmichael," Parker interrupted, giving me a swift kick to the ankle when I opened my mouth again to protest. Trish swiftly wrote my name on the check in elegant script, then folded it in half and pushed it into my hand.

"Vivian, please know that there are plenty of women that could use your help. You've been kind, discreet and sensitive. Not to mention incredibly good at what I asked you to do. If you don't mind, I'd like to refer a couple of my friends to you."

I could see that Parker was winding up for another kick to my ankle, so I nodded reluctantly. "That's very nice of you."

"It's nothing compared to what you've done for me. How may I tell them to reach you?"

"Well, ah...you can just have them call the shop, give them one of our business cards. And if we're not here, tell them to leave a message asking Vivian or Parker to call them back."

Trish reached over and swept the entire stack of business cards we had sitting by the register into her purse. "I'll do that. Thank you again, Vivian, I'll never forget your kindness." She tucked her purse under her arm and, with one last sad smile, was gone.

Parker, Gran and I stared at each other in silence before Parker finally spoke. "I'm not going to say I told you so..."

"Please don't."

"But on your first day back here, *you* were the one who told me that in your experience, what you need to do will often land in your lap. You'd have to be blind to not see this as an opportunity."

"Until I run through all the adultery cases in Savannah."

"Oh, people are always cheating on something, not just on their spouses," Gran finally spoke up. "How much did she give you?"

I'd forgotten about the check in my hand, and when I unfolded it I almost dropped it to the floor in shock. "Uh...two thousand dollars."

Parker's jaw dropped. "For those few hours of work we did?"

"Yeah, wow. And yes, it's half yours."

"No way, you did all the work."

"I just did the driving."

"Girls," Gran cut in. "I'm going to agree with Parker here. Vivian, you have a unique gift, and it would be foolish to waste it. Unless you miraculously learn how to work with flowers, or suddenly love tutoring, throwing away this opportunity will be the single greatest regret you have in your life."

"You want me to go work for a private investigator?"

She arched a delicate silver eyebrow. "*Work for*? No, silly girl, you've made it clear that you're meant to be working for yourself."

Chapter Four

That night, after we collapsed back in our apartment, Parker waited only thirty seconds before taking the bull by the horns. "You know Gran is right."

"She usually is."

"Think about it…you could form your own private investigation agency, take only the cases you want to, handle them the way you know best. And Jesus, V, two thousand dollars for a few hours' work? Give me one good reason why you should turn money like that down."

I shrugged helplessly. "I can't."

"Exactly."

I sighed and leaned over to where my laptop sat on the coffee table. "It's probably not that easy. I can't work under the table for that kind of money forever, and I'm probably not qualified."

"I've never seen 'Private Investigation' as a class at any school, anywhere." She scooted over and looked over my shoulder as I did an internet search for Georgia private investigator requirements. "Oh…okay, I was wrong."

Though I didn't want to admit it, the little bubble of hope that had been forming in my chest was rapidly deflating. Private investigators had to be licensed in Georgia, and there *was* an education requirement, not to mention a decent required amount of start-up capital in the bank, if you wanted to start your own business. The requirements were less restrictive if you chose to work for an established company, but there was no way in hell I was going that route...if they tried to send me on jobs that would raise eyebrows at the CIA, I'd probably be fired for refusing to take them.

Parker squeezed next to me on the couch, absentmindedly tapping her nails against the wood table. "I refuse to accept defeat. Let's work through this...okay, your major was in..."

"Russian and Eurasian Studies. Minor in Psychology."

"Okay, so that's kind of meeting the requirements."

"Not really. P..."

"And I know you still have plenty of cash from your salary over the years piled up, even after your buy-in for Pistils, so that's not an issue."

I didn't even bother protesting, she was on a roll and determined.

"Then you have training, continuing education, and you meet all the other criteria. I'm sure if you told them you'd worked for the CIA, they'd agree to let you apply and there's no way you wouldn't get certified."

"I *can't* tell them I worked for the CIA. Giant hole in resume, remember?"

"Are you sure? I mean, I know you can't tell them anything you actually did, but they'd probably understand that."

"I'm sure."

She cocked her head thoughtfully. "Well, what about going back to school, then? I'm sure tons of your credits would transfer, and you could have a degree in Criminal Justice or whatever in no time."

As much as I loved learning, the thought of going back to school wasn't an appealing one to me at that moment. "I don't know. I'll think about it. I promise."

"Okay," she replied softly. "It's just that this..." she waved her hand at my laptop screen, "This is not insurmountable, and it could absolutely be a career for you."

I knew that she was right, but the disappointment that had pricked the hope bubble in my chest was greater than her enthusiasm at the moment. If everything I wanted to do with my life was going to be undercut by those bastards at Langley, then I might as well stick to tutoring and writing out thank-you cards.

Despite the feeling of utter defeat that followed me to bed, I couldn't turn off my brain. I'd been trained to analyze, to problem-solve, and to keep pushing until the results I wanted were in hand. And although I knew I should dismiss the private investigation option outright, I slowly admitted to myself that I didn't want to. I'd *enjoyed* chasing down and documenting Mr. Rockingham's sins.

That sweet sensation of success that I'd first savored as a case officer had come roaring back with a vengeance.

I'd always thought that I'd be a career officer, it had never crossed my mind that I would voluntarily leave the CIA for anything else. What could even remotely measure up to something that pulled you in so deeply that it became your life, not just a job? Even now, working with two of the three people I loved more than anything in the world, there was a deep ugly vein of dissatisfaction that slid silently through me, one that I felt too guilty to admit aloud.

I'd lived long enough doing something I loved to recognize that nothing would ever really replace it. But private investigation might sure come damn close.

By morning, I'd made up my mind, and told Parker I'd see her at Pistils later. She just nodded and didn't ask any questions, so I waited twenty minutes after she left before I pulled together every scrap of courage I had left and headed out.

My hands-down favorite instructor at The Farm, where I'd received the majority of my CIA training, was a man named Charlie Baumgartner. "The Bomb," as he was nicknamed, taught weapons courses in addition to tradecraft, and he'd earned the nickname as he wouldn't hesitate to go off on any trainee that he felt wasn't taking the classes seriously enough. He was also physically intimidating at 6'5, still a walking tower of muscle even after retiring from active duty with the Special Activities Division twenty years prior. His gruff retorts and perpetual frown terrified pretty much everyone, but I'd discerned after a couple of weeks that he genuinely cared about every single trainee that passed through his care, and he'd stay up all night helping you with whatever you needed, as long as you worked up the nerve to ask.

I respected the hell out of him, and had him to thank for honing my firearms skills down to a point where they'd saved my life more than once.

I'd heard through the grapevine that he'd retired not long after I'd been sent to Bulgaria, and had established his own gun store in his hometown of Statesboro, only an hour from Savannah. After getting the exact address online, I headed up I-16, praying the entire way that this wasn't one of the biggest mistakes of my new life. I wasn't sure I could stand any more kicks in the teeth courtesy of Agency politics and bullshit.

When I arrived, it was early enough that the parking lot held only one other car. I wiped my sweating hands on my jeans, took a deep breath, and headed inside.

Charlie was behind the counter, instantly aware of when I came through the door, and it was only a split-second before recognition dawned across his deeply-tanned face. "Vivian Carmichael. Jesus H. Christ."

"Hi, Charlie," I said cautiously.

"I'll be goddamned." He came from around the

counter. "Good to see you, girl."

I smiled, took a deep breath and extended my right hand. "It's been a long time."

"Sure as hell has. Aww fuck it, c'mere." Two burly arms reached out to wrap me in a strong hug, and I felt tears of relief threaten to make an appearance. I hadn't realized until just then that I'd completely expected to be told to get the hell out of his store. Instead, he gave me one last squeeze and then pulled away, keeping both hands on my shoulders, a rare smile creating wrinkles around his eyes. I didn't go around looking for daddy surrogates, but after Matthew Chase, I'd have chosen Charlie if given the option.

"Here, let me lock the door, then let's sit down. I thought I was seeing a ghost when you walked in here." He reached the entrance in a few strides and flipped the sign to Closed, before slamming the interior door shut and twisting the heavy deadbolts into place.

"Well, I'm a metaphorical ghost, I guess. I don't know if you heard..."

"Hell yes, I heard, everyone heard." He gestured for me to follow him into the back of the store, where the familiar smell of Hoppes #9 took me back in time. There was a giant workbench with every bit and bob a gunsmith might need tucked neatly into its place, a sight almost identical to his personal workshop at The Farm. At his gesture, we sat on two creaking folding chairs that flanked a small portable television. "And everyone knows it was total bullshit too. Toller's a bureaucratic weasel and Fleming is just as bad. After all the risks you took, the danger you were put in, to burn you like that..." He shook his head. "The CIA is your family, until *they* decide they don't want you anymore. Some family."

"To say the least."

"Do you need a job? Because if you do, it's yours if you can run a cash register."

I smiled. "I do need a job, but I'm living in Savannah now. I own a flower shop with my best friend and her grandmother."

"Hell, first a travel agency and now a flower shop? Girl, you never cease to amaze me."

"Well, I don't have much to do with the flowers. I'm the delivery driver."

Charlie let out a long bark of laughter. "Any of your training come in handy?"

"You'd be surprised...I've had to outrun a dog or two, and have employed many driving maneuvers of questionable legality. So yes, it's definitely come in handy. I'm also doing some language tutoring."

"That all sounds like a list of odd jobs, not a career."

"Exactly. And that's why I'm here...I need some career advice."

He leaned back in his chair, brown eyes trained

sharply on mine. "You've got it. Fire away."

"Very long story short, I ended up doing a favor for one of the shop's customers. Busted her cheating husband, I gave her the photos and she gave me a check for two grand."

"Better pay rate than government work, that's for sure."

I nodded. "My best friend..."

"Parker?"

"How can you possibly remember that?"

"I don't forget the best students I trained, and you were definitely right on up there. Plus, I didn't last this long by being forgetful."

That was fair enough, and true. "Are you still married to Christine?"

He pointed a finger at me. "See? You remember things. And no, we got divorced a few years back. We're both better off for it. But back to you."

"So the wronged wife and Parker are both adamant that I look into private investigation, but I looked up the requirements and I don't think I'll be able to meet them. To work on my own, not for someone else."

"Hmm." He reached into his shirt pocket for a pack of cigarettes, a thoughtful look pulling his brows together. "Mind if I smoke?"

"Go ahead."

He tapped the pack and shuffled a cigarette out,

lighting it and blowing a lungful of smoke at the ceiling before speaking again. "Remind me what you majored in again?"

"Russian and Eurasian Studies."

"Well, the major won't do you much good for that, but I'm guessing you want to know if you can bank on your CIA experience to equal things out. You got money?"

"Yes."

He shrugged. "Well, there's a fifty-fifty chance that your training and work experience with the CIA will cancel out the lack of one of the required majors."

"That's the thing...am I even allowed to put that on my resume?"

A rough chuckle rumbled out of his chest. "Let me guess...Toller put the fear of God into you, told you that you can't tell *anyone* what you were doing that whole time, right?"

"Yes, and I..."

"Carmichael, go turn on any television set and you'll see interviews with ex-employees of the CIA. You can read books written by ex-employees, redacted all to hell, but with their real name stamped on the cover. As long as you don't go into any details about exactly what you did, you most certainly *can* put it on your resume. Now whether or not you *want* to, well that's a different story. Are you afraid of retaliation?"

"Bingo."

"Well, I can't promise you that won't happen, and it wouldn't be official and public either; they won't give you a chance to tell your side of the story on CNN. They shot your life to pieces once, there's a chance they *might* do it again. But with all this mess going on in the Middle East right now, and that fool in the White House, they've got bigger things to worry about. My suggestion to you is you be as transparent and matter-of-fact about it as you can. Any employer in that kind of field won't bother asking you exactly what you did, because they know you won't tell them. No, I think the worst that could happen would be if the state calls to confirm your employment there, and they deny ever knowing you."

That was something I hadn't even thought of, I'd been more worried about tipping the Agency off that I was going public with my past employment and then getting sued, jailed, or wiped off the face of the planet altogether.

"Well, as in most things in life, it's all in who you know. And I happen to know the current president of GAPPI...that's one of the professional organizations here in Georgia. I could give him a call, see what he thinks. And I'll vouch for you too...CIA training and experience stomp a diploma any day, that's just a piece of paper. Maybe they'll take my word for it instead of calling to check your employment."

Relief flooded through me, cool and sweet. "Thank you."

"Don't mention it, you paid me back in advance by not being a raging pain in my ass during training. So private investigation...I dabbled in it myself a bit before I realized that being built like a brick shithouse doesn't help you blend in. I do a few personal security gigs here and there, mostly for folks up in Atlanta. But you'll do fine. Got equipment?"

"I was waiting to see if I could even apply before I started dropping money into the business."

He grunted. "Smart. But *when*, not if, you're set up and legal, you get back up here and I'll set you up. Not just with that pansy bullshit anyone can buy...I've got a few contacts of my own, and I have some Agency equipment that would make their hair curl if they knew about it."

"I knew I came to the right place."

"Sure as hell did. All right, let's talk about getting this whole thing going."

Chapter Five

By the time I made it back to Pistils, it was almost closing time, and both Parker and Gran were visibly relieved to see me.

"Not that we don't trust you to take care of yourself, sweetpea," Gran said, patting my cheek, "But give us a call next time."

"I'm sorry." The visit with Charlie had stretched into hours as he'd closed his store for the day, and in between phone calls and making lists, he'd slipped back into training mode. My head was swirling with all the information he'd drilled into me.

"We figured it was something important, and it was a slow day," Parker reassured me. "It was pretty much all walk-in traffic."

"Yeah, but I should have let you know, I'm sorry."

"Then you can make it up to me by closing up, how's that?" Gran offered. "There's a book club at that little shop right down the street, I was going to drop in and see if they're taking new members."

"Yes, absolutely. Go."

"Do you want me to pick you up afterward?" Parker flipped off the radio we kept behind the counter.

"Oh no, I'll just move my car right down there, and head home after. You girls finish up and then go home...no, better yet, go do something fun. Meet some nice young men."

I couldn't help but laugh as Gran bustled out the door. "She didn't like Daniel, huh?"

"Not so much. It's okay, he came into the shop today and didn't pass the Gran Test. I'm not even going to bother subjecting him to the Carmichael Inquisition."

"What was wrong with him?"

"He just wasn't Mr. Right." Parker grabbed the broom as I began wiping off the counters. "So...where'd you go today?"

"Statesboro...it's about an hour northwest of here. One of my old trainers has a business there, and I needed some advice. He was sort of like a mentor to me."

"Yeah?"

"I ran the private investigation thing by him...some of the things you and I talked about last night."

I could tell Parker was dying to get the whole story, but she kept sweeping, playing it cool. "And?"

"He thinks it's doable. I mean, I still have to go through the application and training and all that, but he's got a few strings he's willing to pull on my behalf."

Now Parker did stop sweeping. "So you're going to do it?"

"I'm going to try."

She dropped the broom this time and hopped across the shop to me, pulling me into a bone-crushing hug. "That's awesome! And you'll be amazing, pulling in all that rich-people money in no time. No more flower deliveries for you!"

"Well, I actually wanted to talk to you about that," I laughed. "Charlie...my friend...he and I both agree that even though I would be completely legal if everything goes through, that I probably shouldn't be super-visible with the business. The CIA might be okay with me just mentioning that I once worked there so that I can get licensed, but I don't need to flaunt it as a form of advertising. So I'll probably be doing word-of-mouth only, and I'd like to keep working here too."

She nodded, leaning against the counter. "That makes sense. So Pistils would be a cover business for you?"

"Well, sort of. It's a completely legal business, and would continue to be. The private investigation business would be an entirely separate entity, but also legal. I'm not required to advertise if I don't want to. I think the word-of-mouth aspect will actually make it even more appealing...you have to know someone who knows. It will add to our credibility as being discreet."

"*Our*?" Parker's eyebrows went up.

"That was the other thing I wanted to ask you. You kept up with me no problem last week, and that's with zero training or experience, aside from when we busted Shane. And you seemed to enjoy it. So I swear I won't be offended if you say no, but...I was wondering if you'd like to go in with me, as my partner."

I barely got the last word out before she had me in another hug, this one even tighter than before. "Yes! Oh my God, yes! I wanted to ask you, but I was afraid that I'd sound stupid...I have zero experience and..."

"On paper, your degree has more weight than mine does," I grinned. "And we can go through the training and everything together. Then we'll have our own business, busting the jerks of the world while slinging flowers on the side. Gran is going to be so proud."

Parker shook her head, her smile brighter than I'd seen it in a long time. "You're kidding, right? This is *Gran* we're talking about. She's probably going to want to get in on the action too."

Chapter Six

I'd known that Charlie would be an asset of immense value, but even I was shocked when, three days after my visit, he called and told to fill out the application and send everything to him, that he'd take care of getting it through to the right people. And that in the meantime, I'd better have my ass in Statesboro three days a week for training.

Those days were like CIA training on steroids. I wouldn't go so far as to call Charlie's gun shop a cover, but he also did a brisk business supplying professional-level spy equipment to people he trusted, mostly ex-CIA, NSA and even a few FBI veterans. The amateur-level crap for the public was in the front of the store. He and I took turns taking care of walk-in customers, while in the meantime we were putting together an arsenal that was a private investigator's wet dream. Tiny cameras, bugs, software, log-ins to databases...and even things that I hadn't known about while active in the field.

"Who are you getting all this stuff from?" I asked him on the second day.

"Let me put it this way: I'll tell him that if I die, you can take my place, and you'll find out then."

"You make it sound like arms dealing," I grumbled.

"No shit," he snapped back, tossing a cable in my

direction. "What do you think half this gear is? Just because it doesn't shoot bullets doesn't make it any less dangerous...or useful."

"Gotcha."

After a long talk, Parker and I agreed that I'd train her after Charlie put me through the wringer, then we both sat down to tell Gran.

"Well just be careful, sweetpeas," she sighed, sitting back at her polished desk in Pistils' back room. "I'm not worried about you taking care of yourselves...either of you...but there are some mean people in the world."

My best friend and I exchanged a glance. We'd spent hours talking into the night about how we'd run the business. "There are going to be people calling here to set up, uh, services, Gran. Are you okay with that? Just get their names and numbers."

Gran shot her granddaughter a withering look. "I'm more than capable of answering the phone and taking messages, you know."

"That's not what I..."

"I know, I know," she huffed. "All right, tell me what I should know."

I smothered a smile. "If they call and ask for me or Parker to call them back, but don't mention anything about flowers, get their name and number and tell them we'll get back to them."

Gran frowned. "Wouldn't it be easier and faster if

I got some of the details from them on the phone?"

"We don't want you to have to..."

"I *want* to," she interrupted again. "At least I know that my James never cheated on me, but infidelity seems to be the thing to do these days. I'd rather help you nail those cheating bastards to the wall. Oh, and the floozies too, can't forget about them."

I was laughing silently as Parker frowned at her grandmother. "Gran..."

"Not to mention the thieves and the swindlers and...it's not like I died once I hit seventy, you know. I need a bit more excitement in my life."

Parker turned to look at me with giant eyes, and I shrugged. "I don't have a problem with it."

"Well I do!"

"Parker Marie Chase! I'm not quite sure why you're so wound up about this. Now if I start wanting to tote a gun like Vivian and asking to go along on stakeouts, then maybe you can start worrying. But as it is now, I'm more than capable of handling the administrative side of *both* our businesses."

"Fine," Parker grumbled, and I did my best to cover my surprise that Gran knew I'd gotten a concealed carry license. The past few years of my life had completely destroyed any trust I had in humanity.

"Now Vivian, you just fill out a form with what information you want me to ask them, and we'll be all ready to go once you're open for business."

That night, the burner phone rang.

It had sat there, on my bedside table, for days that turned to weeks that turned to months. More than once, I'd almost given up, almost let the battery run down or dropped it in a glass of water. But just as I still thought of David every single day, every night, I remembered his words to me. *"Keep it on, all the time."*

Caution had been drilled into me, though, so I picked it up with shaking fingers and hit the green button to answer the call. I lifted it to my ear and waited in silence.

"Privet, moya dorogaya."

At the sound of his voice, my knees buckled and I sagged onto the bed. Of course he would choose Russian to greet me, to reassure me that this was a safe connection. "Is everything okay?"

"Everything is fine, Viv, I just needed to hear your voice tonight." He sounded exhausted. "I'll fully admit to being selfish."

"You don't hear me complaining." My mind whirled. "Are you allowed to tell me where you are?"

"I just left Grozny, tying up some loose ends."

I swallowed hard, forcing back memories of the Chechen city and what I'd done there. Both the best and worst acts of my career. "Mutual friends of ours?"

"A few. You'd be amazed at who's still out and about."

"It's probably better that I don't know."

"Agreed. How are you Viv?"

"Things are going really well here. Better than I'd expected."

"Keeping your nose clean?"

"Asks the man who's currently in *Chechnya*."

That got a short laugh out of him. "Fair enough."

I exhaled carefully. "Are you really okay?"

"I will be, now that I know you're doing well. I miss you."

"I miss you too." My voice caught. "It doesn't change anything, though."

"I wasn't expecting it to. Hoping, yes."

"I wish I could change everything. You know I do."

"I know." He sounded sad. "We both would, in a heartbeat. But I'm a patient man."

"What are you waiting for specifically?" *Me.*

"Scandals die quickly, and yours was, regardless of it being due to a bloody tragedy, fairly minor. Give it a couple of administration changes and your name will just be a blip in Agency history. Then if you feel safe enough being around me, we'll decide what we're doing. Although maybe I'm assuming too much..."

"No," I interrupted quickly. "That hasn't changed.

I just wish I shared your optimism about turning into an Agency blip. They've got long memories there."

"You still think you're poison. Toxic." It wasn't a question.

"Undoubtedly."

"Viv, you aren't..."

"Stop. Please. I can't have this conversation again. It almost killed me the last time."

"I'm sorry," he said after a moment. "I keep telling myself that I need to let you go, to let you rebuild a life and be happy. But I don't want that...I want you to be happy with *me*." His Scottish brogue was more pronounced than I'd ever heard it. "I think about you and me at Bonnyrigg all the time."

"There's still a hold on my passport."

"I know. I checked." He took a deep breath. "But there isn't one on mine."

"David, don't. You know they're keeping tabs on me. Farming it out to some first year rookie officers, probably."

"Well then I'll keep tabs on you myself. And when they stop, I'll be there. You aren't Aldrich fucking Ames, Viv, just stay out of Bulgaria and I promise you, things will fade in time."

"Not everything fades."

"For our sake, I sincerely hope not. I won't keep you on the line any longer, but remember that I love you, and I will always be there for you if you need me. *Ty nuzhna mnye*."

"*Vsegda*," I replied softly. *Always*.

"Goodbye Viv."

"Goodbye." I hung up the burner and dropped it with nerveless fingers onto the bed. Hearing his voice had brought everything back. His touch, the warmth of his body, his kisses, the way he held me down when I was sure the world was determined to spin me off into space. The way he'd made me feel safe, the plans we'd made. It all came roaring back in that moment, as if it had all happened only hours ago instead of months. I'd been more right than I knew...not everything faded.

Vsegda.

I was sure I had Charlie to thank for more than I'd ever know, but the license for having our own private investigation company went through without a hitch, although it drained both our savings accounts and then some. Luckily, I'd been taking low-risk cases under the table while we completed all the basic requirements, and word spread quickly when we were legal and officially open for business.

Pistils business cards were passed from hand to manicured hand, discreetly, under tables and in powder rooms. *Just call and ask for Parker or Vivian to call you back.* Within the first six months, we'd done everything from busting nannies with sticky fingers to small business workers comp fraud to our overwhelming bread-and-butter...infidelity. We were called to court twice to testify on cases, and I'd been ridiculously proud of my best friend when Parker was cooler than a cucumber even while being grilled by an overzealous divorce lawyer.

P&V, Inc. was a thing, a real thing. And even as we started replacing our startup money, Pistils' popularity continued to skyrocket, yet another positive omen.

It should have been enough. And in some ways, it *was* enough. I was with two of the people I loved best in the world, doing something that my mind and body had been carefully shaped through years of training and experience to do. We were happy, we were safe, and that was what should always matter in the end.

Right?

Vsegda.

Every day, every night, *vsegda* was what I reminded myself, along with *ya nadeyus...I hope.*

A Note from the Author

Hello friends! I hope you enjoyed this introductory novella to the *Pistils* Series! If so, it would mean the world to me if you would **consider leaving a review** on Amazon, B&N, iBooks, and **a Goodreads review** would be an amazing plus as well (you can just copy and paste your other review)! Also feel free to mention that the e-book is a <u>permanently-free download</u>!

I dedicated this novella in part to indie book readers, because YOU are the reason we keep sharing the worlds we build with you! YOU are the ones who leave reviews and make recommendations that help us to grow!

If you're interested in following Vivian and Parker into the world they're just starting to plunge into, come on over to **TwintypeBooks.com**, which will give you all your buying platform options!

While there, I also hope you'll consider signing up for my mailing list...I call it "**all the good stuff**," because you'll get advance notice of book releases, events, blog posts, and even sales/coupon codes! No spam, no sharing of your info, it's just the good stuff. And, should you so choose, you can unsubscribe at any time.

THANK YOU for starting this adventure, I hope you'll continue on!

About the Author

Kate McNeil is a writer, reader, photographer, knitter and movie critic. She is a Kentucky girl who currently lives in Metro Detroit with her husband.

Sneak Peek

Okay, okay, you didn't think I'd just quit *there*, did you?? Please enjoy this sneak peek at the next book in the series: *Pistils!*

Chapter One – Vivian

"You have a new case, dearie."

The corners of my mouth curled up reluctantly. No matter how many times I'd heard those words come from Gran's sweet little mouth, it always cracked me up. She may have looked every inch the elderly southern lady of leisure, but Gran hadn't retired, not by a long shot.

"What is it?"

"Possible cheating husband, wife is the client," she rattled off, barely looking at the sheet covered with hand-scrawled notes before her. "Lots of money involved, plus a prenup. Big names. Absolute discretion, of course."

"Of course," I echoed her. "Anyone we'd recognize?"

Gran fluttered a blue-veined hand in the air, sharp eyes peering over her spectacles. "Jackson and Lisa Piedmont."

"The Piedmonts?" I repeated, lifting my eyebrows. Everyone in Savannah knew who the Piedmont family was; they were the next generation of old money, charity balls, and society pages. Oh, and the fact that Randall Piedmont, Jackson's father, was a United States senator for the state of Georgia. *Damn.* Parker and I had worked for plenty of high-profile and wealthy clients since starting our two-woman private investigation business, but a senator's daughter-in-law was something else entirely. "Lisa wants us? Don't they have enough money to, oh I don't know, hire some ex-military contracting firm or something?"

"Lisa wants you," Gran stated firmly. "She's convinced Jackson is having an affair, but wants proof before she takes any action. And apparently one of her friends told her about you." She shoved a handful of papers at me. "Here are the details, her contact information, and what I was able to pull off the internet about both of them. I told her you two would meet with her this afternoon, and she's expecting you at three-thirty sharp."

Having been summarily dismissed from Gran's office, I took a deep breath and headed up to the front of our florist shop. Pistils. There were very few people who knew about or appreciated the humor in our choice of name for our cover business, and the customers who only came in for flowers and balloons certainly had no idea. The shop itself was the epitome of cheer and color, and enormous front windows let in plenty of daylight, showing off the rainbow of floral displays to their best advantage. The hardwood floor gleamed and the soft off-white walls were the perfect backdrop. It had been a flower shop before we'd bought it, but we had transformed it into something else entirely, and it was one of our two greatest accomplishments.

Parker was right where I expected her to be, humming happily to a tune on the iPod we had plugged in behind the counter, the pink tips on her blonde hair bobbing as she bounced to the music. In front of her was a gorgeous vase filled with roses. Arranging flowers was a knack she'd apparently inherited from Gran, a very fortunate thing since plants and I didn't exactly get along. Parker usually relegated me to writing out the note cards and making deliveries, and for good reason.

I sighed softly at seeing my best friend in such an obviously good mood. I was always reluctant to tell Parker that we had another cheating case, even though they made up seventy-five percent of our business. Along with crooked employees and attempted hitman-hirings, they were our bread-and-butter. But I always did dread it, since I knew that every single cheating case reminded her of the past, even if just a little.

Parker was the ultimate romantic at heart, and in the very best way possible. The sweet outgoing kind girl she'd been in high school had grown into an empathetic woman who still believed in happily-ever-afters, the romance of grand gestures, and that it was perfectly acceptable and expected to hold out for commitment until your soul mate came along. The fact that someone had almost knocked all of that out of her was still enough to make me see red.

It was, in the long run, the reason we'd gone into private investigation.

Three years ago, Parker's gut had told her that

Shane, an asshole I'd never liked, might be stepping out on her. I'd just returned from Langley and, not being in the most charitable state of mind toward anyone, let alone him, suggested we nose around. Just to put her mind at ease, of course. After all, they'd been together for five and a half years.

We'd found out two things. One, Shane was a two-timing snake who was so used to cheating on my best friend, he'd gotten slightly careless in covering it up. Two, we discovered that we were remarkably good at finding things. Like, scary good.

I guess it shouldn't have been surprising, with my years of working as a CIA case officer and Parker's unerringly good gut instincts. Since moving to Savannah over two years ago, ostensibly to buy out a struggling flower shop, we'd slowly built up quite a respectable business. We were discreet, efficient and, above all, good. P&V, Inc. wasn't in the Yellow Pages, however. Oh no. You had to know someone who knew us. Socialites, locally-based celebrities, athletes, and members of ladies' clubs...they would discreetly slip their friends a Pistils business card while clueing them in on the magic words: "Ask for Parker or Vivian to call you back." Our clientele was overwhelmingly female, but we'd had our fair share of men seeking help too. Our results built respect.

Now, since Pistils was operating in the black, and P&V, Inc. was able to charge more-than-decent nonrefundable rates, all three of us were doing just fine. Gran had her own cottage close to all the social activities she enjoyed, while Parker and I shared a comfortable apartment east of downtown. We were in a good place all the way around, there was no denying it.

"Hey you." I slid onto one of the stools we kept behind the counter. "New case. Gran already set us up an appointment and everything."

"She's the best thing we brought with us from Charleston." Parker grinned and reached back to turn down the volume on the music. "Details?"

I made my voice as neutral as possible; this was just business, after all. "Possible cheating, big money, big names. Wife is the client."

I saw a shadow pass across my best friend's eyes, but it was gone in a moment as she slipped into PI mode. "Who is it?"

"Jackson and Lisa Piedmont."

Parker whistled softly. "That'll be a touchy one. Lisa thinks he's fooling around? Couldn't she just have the Secret Service tail him or something?"

"Senators and their families don't normally have Secret Service privileges," I said absently, glancing over Gran's notes again. "We have an appointment with her at three-thirty, at their place. According to Gran we're supposedly there to discuss floral arrangements for his parents' fiftieth wedding anniversary. Which *is* legitimate, we picked up that gig too. It's at the Grantham House in a few weeks."

"That's cutting it pretty tight, we'll need to sit down and plan as soon as we have details. Three-thirty, huh? I can have these done by then if you'll help me clean up." Her blue eyes slipped back over to the roses. "Let's get to it."

~*~

Precisely two minutes before our scheduled appointment, Parker and I pulled up to the Piedmonts' home in the Pistils delivery van. It wasn't quite a historic district mansion like Jackson's parents', but he and Lisa lived in an expensive gated community just west of downtown, where sprawling green lawns and carefully-manicured flower beds were de rigueur.

"I still don't get it," Parker had muttered, as we pulled away from the guard shack after being checked against the approved visitors list. "I mean, we're good, but why us?"

I'd shrugged. I was still surprised myself that a member of what was arguably Savannah's most wealthy and prominent old families had singled us out for a case of this magnitude. A Piedmont divorce would be huge news, and there was always a chance we would be called to testify in court. This was the kind of thing you'd want the biggest, best, and most expensive private investigators on. But hell, you never knew and I wasn't one to wonder...too much. "Maybe she's more comfortable with two young women. Maybe whoever referred us really sang our praises. Who knows?"

"Good point." Parker swung the van into the long driveway of the gorgeous home. "Shall we?"

Both of us were wearing all-white, except for the Pistils logo on the front of our perfectly-starched expensive polos. We looked fresh as daisies, pretty as buttercups. I left my .45 under the seat. I never went anywhere without it; it was a risky business we were in after all. It didn't exactly match my work uniform, though.

Lisa Piedmont herself answered the glorious doorbell. We both recognized her immediately from grainy society news photos as well as the pictures Gran had printed off the internet. Of course those hadn't included black splotches of mascara under her eyes and the tears that had streaked her foundation. Even through that, you could tell that she was an attractive woman, in her own way. Long blonde hair with expensive highlights, a slim toned body, and a smooth tan. If she'd had any work done, the plastic surgeon had done an excellent job making it look natural. She gave us a wobbly smile and we followed her inside.

"I just don't know what to do!" she burst out after we were settled in the front room, or the parlor, or whatever it was the rich called it. "I know he's having an affair, I just know it! But I don't know what to do!" Then she completely broke down into sobs.

Parker and I exchanged a glance. We'd dealt with plenty of hysterical wives in our short career, and established that she was much more empathetic and able to comfort women than I'd ever be able to. I could play the role if I needed to, but were it up to me, I'd take the route of slapping her and telling her to pull herself together. I had very little patience for histrionics.

My best friend moved over to the couch next to the wailing Lisa and put her arm around her shoulders. "Mrs. Piedmont, listen, I know you're upset. But I need you to take a few deep breaths and then answer a question or two, okay? Can you do that for us?"

Lisa's blotchy face quivered. "I'll try."

"Okay, that's all we ask. First off, is there anyone in the house besides us right now? Anyone you don't want overhearing this conversation?"

She shook her head, blonde hair now sticking to her wet cheeks. "I sent the housekeeper out on a bunch of errands."

Of course you did, I thought, before mentally chastising myself. Making assumptions or judgments about the client was not appropriate or professional.

"All right then," Parker soothed, and once again I found myself in awe of her. She really was the nicest person I knew. "Why don't you start from the beginning, and we'll work from there?"

Lisa drew in a deep shaking breath. "It's just, I don't know, a gut feeling? He's so distant, I don't think he really even likes me anymore. And we haven't, um, we haven't had sex in forever, so..."

Parker patted her shoulder. "We understand. Keep going."

"Just...all those things you read about in magazines, how to know if your man is cheating on you? Jack fits all of those!" Lisa looked ready to break down again. "I really thought we were happy, but I guess he was happier with someone else."

"What kinds of things?" Parker encouraged.

"He works all the time. I know he's busy, he's an architect with his own firm. But now he spends all his time there, sometimes he even sleeps at the office! When he is here, he's distant. We don't talk. He doesn't seem to care about me or my interests at all anymore. We don't do anything together. And as I mentioned, our love life is completely non-existent now."

"About how long ago did this start?"

"Oh, a few months ago, maybe?"

My turn. "It sounds like a solid place for us to start from, Mrs. Piedmont, we just need you to tell us exactly what you want." Parker was definitely the better people-person, but I tended to be the hard-ass when it came to having them spell out what they were hiring us for and then committing to it. We weren't there as therapists, after all.

Lisa blotted her red face with a tissue. "I just need to know. I want proof. I can't live *not* knowing one way or the other." Her face crumpled again. "I just need to see it with my own eyes."

Parker and I exchanged glances once more; Lisa was still being too vague. We needed to know exactly what was expected of us, and how far she wanted us to go. "Mrs. Piedmont, we can follow your husband, check up on his activities, and document them accordingly. But we always ask up front, just so we know what we're getting into...if we find admissible evidence that he's cheating, will you want us to testify in court, should you choose to divorce him?"

Her pink lips quivered. "I hate to think of it, but if he's cheating on me, I just can't stay with him. I can't. I love him but I couldn't get past something like that. So yes, anything you find, if it comes to that, I'll need that to back me up."

I lifted my eyebrows at Parker, and she shrugged. There was no reason for us not to take the case. And once again, I got to be the hard-ass, a role I'd played so many times before. "We'll take your case, Mrs. Piedmont. Let's go through our contract, and take it from there."

~*~

Parker and I were both sunk in our own thoughts as we left the Piedmont residence. Lisa had signed the contract and immediately written a personal check without a single reservation about our terms or rates. We had our mark. And yet...

"What did you think?" I finally broke the silence.

Parker pursed her lips. "I want to believe her. I can't help but think she's just going for guilt, though...like if she caught him cheating, she might be furious or devastated, but she might not necessarily divorce him. Hell, it would be diamonds and St. Lucia every year if she rode him hard enough about it."

This was why Parker and I worked so perfectly together, our gut instincts were usually right on. "I wonder which one she loves more, Jackson or his money? Or both equally?"

"I could see it either way," Parker said thoughtfully. "I mean, she was obviously upset. Who wouldn't be? But having him by the balls and getting all the goodies and being able to privately keep him in check...I just can't shake that it might be the angle she's playing."

"Except she flat out said she would want a divorce." I rubbed my forehead. "Unless she plans on having a sudden change of heart even if we get pictures of him with his pants around his ankles."

"Good point."

"We've got our work cut out for us, then. "I'll get to work on tracking Jackson, you want to find out what he's been up to over the past few months?"

Parker flashed me her trademark cheerful smile. "I'm on it."

Chapter Two - **Parker**

Three Years Ago...

Vivian and I sat in front of my laptop, staring at the screen thoughtfully as I tapped my nails against the plastic. I knew without a shadow of a doubt that I wanted to do this, to mortify and shame him like he'd done me. The crux of the matter was that I'd never done anything so underhanded.

"That miserable excuse of a human being deserves this, Parker. Don't forget that for a single second."

I let Vivian's words, spoken with so much conviction, seep into my pores and give me the bravery I needed to go through with this. She was going through her own personal turmoil considering her career had just ended with the CIA. She wouldn't give me any other details, but I knew it couldn't have been a good situation. I was just selfishly happy that she was home, because I needed my best friend more than anything. Taking a deep breath, I replayed the last two weeks of my life that had brought me to this very moment.

It all began with a coincidental insult slung at me by a disgruntled woman who was taking my self-defense class. "Just because she can kick ass, she thinks she's a pink Powerpuff Girl now. Well at least the annoying high-pitched voice is accurate."

Familiar words. Eerily familiar.

Words spoken by my boyfriend Shane the night I came home with hot pink tips on my long, blonde hair. I loved them. They made me feel empowered and real. He mocked me. "Just because you know how to beat some ass, you think you're a pink Powerpuff girl now? What was her name anyway, Blossom?"

Their words ate at me, my mind constantly trying to conjure up a way to convince me this was nothing more than a coincidence. But honestly, a Powerpuff Girl? Blossom didn't even have pink hair...

By the time my obsession with finding the truth about the man I had adored for five and a half years became more than I could handle, Vivian was already on her way back to Charleston. She bounded through my front door, throwing her things in the nearest chair and hugging me tight. "You want answers, P? Well...let's find them."

For as much as my heart was breaking, it exhilarated me to no end being able to investigate like that with my best friend. I'd learned so much that night and it was fascinating to see the skill and precision Vivian had acquired in her years with the CIA. From hacking Shane's computer and email passwords with ease to knowing just what to search for in order to discover what he was hiding, I felt like her student, and I was more than eager to learn.

I knew I'd had it in me all along but researching to find the truth, to right a wrong, to truly stand up for myself...as painful as the whole situation was, it made me realize my true calling.

Investigating brought me back to life, even when the only life I'd ever known was falling apart around me.

When one Facebook comment led to a Tumblr account, and a link led to a Twitter account, and that Twitter account led to another link to a WordPress blog, we'd finally found the source of my coincidental situation. All modesty aside, it had nothing to do with luck. Viv and I were unstoppable when we were on a mission.

STUPID SHIT MY GIRLFRIEND DOES

That was the name of his blog. Tears rolled down my cheeks and Vivian slammed her fist against the desktop so hard our wine glasses went flying as we read excerpts of my life with Shane. We cowered at pictures of me sleeping with drool on my chin, my face in a green cleansing mask. And it just kept on going. Me with a giant zit, rat's nest hair, and then I stumbled upon the many heartless lists he made for fun.

"Girls I'd rather nail than Parker"

"Shane's awesome list of things he'd rather do than listen to his girlfriend speak"

"Shane's top ten lies to feed your woman to get what you want"

Then of course there was the section where his

111

pig-headed, disgusting followers could submit questions.

The majority of them asked things that made me sick, and Shane's equally disturbing replies had me questioning how I had existed with this man for almost six years when he was quite obviously a stranger to me.

Some of his followers were demanding to know how he could do this to a seemingly sweet and very attractive girl. "Because I can," was his answer.

Why don't you just break up with her? *"When I find a woman hot enough to ditch her for, I will. There's no point leaving when I have a built in housecleaner, clothes washer, dish doer, and a piece of ass when I need it."*

As my best friend held me tight, I'd found the proof I needed. A short blurb that provided the evidence to us, clear as day.

Stupid Shit My Girlfriend Does, Example 103955...
I've Completely Lost Count

So she comes home last night, totally forgetting to pick up the dry cleaning I'd reminded her about that morning, and her hair is pink. Fucking pink. Who does she think she is, a punk? A rebellious teenager? She's almost thirty and looks absolutely ridiculous. I mean, just because she teaches people how to kick ass and she's tiny as hell, she thinks she's a Powerpuff Girl now? That pink one...Blossom. Her high-pitched voice annoyed me to no end which, ironically enough, goes the same for Parker. At least that part is accurate.

So maybe she is that pathetic little Powerpuff Girl, thinking she's hot shit because she has pink hair. But is it a cry for help? A mid-life crisis? Like the forty-year-old dude with a red Corvette, is she just trying to be young again? Whatever... I need to get laid, and the next person riding me will not have pink goddamn hair, of that I can assure you. Peace out!

There it was, in black and white. Vivian wanted to kill him, and considering her background and current temperament, I wasn't quite sure she only meant figuratively. But as the tears ran silently down my cheeks, an eerie calm settled over me. One word, heavy and determined sat on the tip of my tongue. "Revenge. I want revenge, Vivian."

So as I sat there with my finger hovering over the mouse, seconds away from posting every one of his dirty little secrets, I let my hesitation fly out the window. I was a damn good person and this was something I owed to myself, that he owed me after years of slander and cheating and lying straight to my face.

I stared at the computer, ready to share one final post on his blog.

We'd changed all his passwords to something so complex, there was no way in hell he'd ever be getting into it again.

I hit enter.

Nothing had ever felt so sweet.

Stupid Shit I Do, By Parker

1. The laundry of a pathetic cheating bastard who never appreciated how good he had it. Click here and here to see every skid-marked pair of underwear he owns.

2. Fake hundreds upon hundreds of orgasms, letting Shane Montgomery think his manhood was something to write home about. Click here, here, and here to see numerous examples of said manhood, erect and embarrassingly small. Honestly, a baby carrot would have provided me more pleasure.

3. Find incriminating photos on my boyfriend's computer, his hand buried beneath Lilith Stanton's immaculate dress, tongue shoved in her mouth at last year's Christmas party. Who knew he was so talented at taking selfies? Click here to see Shane and the boss's wife rounding second base and on the fast track to third. Oops, I think I emailed these to Mr. James Stanton, president and CEO of the company Shane works for. His wife does look lovely in chiffon.

4. Link every contact in his address book to this little blog, chronicling my idiocy and showcasing just how much of an awesome, big macho man he is. Click <u>here</u> to see Shane cramming his large frame into one of my baby doll lingerie dresses and heels, posing otherwise naked for the camera.

5. The dumbest thing I have ever done is give over five years of my life to a man that has appreciated none of it. I was an idiot for putting his needs before mine, for letting him crush and stifle every beautiful, unique thing about me. And finally, I'm beyond stupid for letting him think I'm anything other than a strong, amazing woman. If you're curious, here is an accurate picture of <u>me</u>, ink peeking out beneath my sleeveless shirt, pink tips bright and fierce as my hair lays long and wavy down my back. If you're wondering why my smile is so wide and the fire in my eyes so bright, it's probably because revenge is just that sweet.

Would a real man do this to a woman? Shane Montgomery is a pathetic excuse for a human being but after all this, I can't really be mad at him.

His ignorance has set me free...

...and I'm more than ready to fly.

Sincerely,

The girl who does stupid shit

Present Day...

I awoke with a start, my head jerking up from the couch cushion with a random piece of paper stuck to my face. This certainly wasn't the first time I'd fallen asleep while investigating our potential bad guy, but waking up to memories of a past that seemed like forever ago wasn't exactly my idea of a good time.

I couldn't understand why thoughts of Shane pummeled me every time we began a new cheating investigation. Cases like these made up the majority of our business, but it never failed to bring forth memories I simply wanted to forget.

It wasn't like I missed Shane, not by a long shot. Truth be told, I was in denial for the last few years of my relationship with him, ignoring the reality of what we were because I just didn't want to acknowledge it. Our first two years together were, for lack of a better and less whimsical word, magic. We were head over heels in love, he treated me like a princess, and even when tragedy struck I was blessed with his love and constant support to get me through the loss of my mother to ovarian cancer. With Vivian out on assignment with no chance of coming home, it was nearly unbearable to experience that kind of devastation without her. If I hadn't had Shane to get me through that time, I don't know how I would have survived.

I could count on one hand how many times my best friend and boyfriend had met one another, and still they couldn't see eye to eye. Thankfully they at least pretended to tolerate each other for my sake, because at the time I'd thought that I needed them both equally as much. I should have listened to Vivian's reservations about Shane, but he practically worshipped the ground I walked on and made me feel so safe. Even after the magic had somehow become lost in our relationship after a handful of years, we still worked well as a team. Maybe I was in a relationship that I knew was ho-hum to both of us, but I was under the pretense that growing up meant sacrificing that puppy dog love.

It turned out that ho-hum to Shane meant three years of cheating and then later publicly humiliating the woman who had stood by his side through thick and thin. So even though he no longer meant anything to me, it was obvious why cheating cases still left a bit of an ache in my bruised and battered heart.

After Señor Douchebag was out of my life and revenge was gratifyingly handed to him, I vowed to always listen to myself, my uncanny intuition, and most of all my raw gut instinct that I had suppressed during my time with Shane.

The real problem was that I was guarding my heart so closely now, afraid I'd be blindsided again by someone I let myself trust. I hadn't had a real date in years even though I'd occasionally found someone to help scratch the itch, but the fear of getting hurt again was the only thing keeping me from opening up completely to another person.

This case certainly wasn't helping matters.

Lisa Piedmont put on quite a show during our first meeting at her lavish home two days ago. While I'd *wanted* to believe her theatrical performance, my instincts were telling me that something wasn't right. Whether she had an ulterior motive or there was a piece of the story that she'd left out, I knew there was something that had yet to be discovered. Unfortunately for me she was not the mark, and instead I was being paid to learn more about Jackson Piedmont.

It was easy enough to find information on his professional life, like his company profile and a few gala pictures featuring him smiling widely and shaking hands with other obviously well-to-do gentlemen. But after researching him relentlessly for the past forty-eight hours, I was hitting every dead end imaginable regarding his personal life.

Dude didn't even have Facebook for crying out loud.

I sighed, running a hand through my hair. As good

as I knew I was at getting to the bottom of things, I needed my other half in order to really function properly, especially with my mind conjuring up unpleasant memories from the past. When Vivian and I got together, we were absolutely unstoppable.

I heard the key in the door and I closed my laptop. "Speak of the devil."

Vivian looked around and gave me a judgy look. "You were speaking to yourself about me? Creepy, P."

I laughed, shaking my head. "Never mind. This computer is frying my brain. Chinese?"

"We should probably make it take-out," she sighed, nodding toward the door. "And you better un-fry your brain, because we have a lot of work to do."

Yep, as usual, it was going to be a late night.

~*~

I'd decided to tag along on our take-out run so Viv and I could go over the timeline for the case. In the past we had come up with some majorly good ideas while driving and talking, but at that moment I was too hungry to even think. I was waiting in the parking lot for Viv to come out with our food so we could book it back home and get to work, when my ringing phone broke the silence of the car. I smiled as I checked the caller ID and saw Gran's face on the screen.

"Hello, is this Parker Chase, Private Investigator Extraordinaire? I have a hot case for you, dear. I can't seem to find my glasses."

I couldn't help but laugh. We wouldn't have been able to leave Charleston if Gran hadn't agreed to come along. Even though I'd been more than ready to leave town and start fresh, my Gran was the light of my life, and we were the last two family members remaining in our hometown. It didn't take much convincing. After telling her our grand plan and insisting we'd need her help for our cover business, she was downright excited to come along. My Gran had run her own florist shop, Black-Eyed Susans, for over forty years. She was more than happy to come out of retirement and help us with the ins and outs of our business.

She was even more excited to help us "nail the cheating bastards of the world to the wall."

"Gran, did you really call me to help you find your glasses?" I chuckled.

"No, honey. I did lose them, but I'm sure they're around here somewhere. I was really wondering if my girls have found anything on the Piedmont case yet."

"Not a thing," I sighed despondently. "Looks like it's going to be a late one. We're actually just grabbing some take-out now, and then it'll be time to put our game faces on."

"I'll open up the shop tomorrow. I figured you'd both be busy with such a high profile case hanging in the balance."

"I don't know what we'd do without you, Gran."

She laughed softly. "Oh honey, doing this with you girls has been the highlight of my very long life. I should be the one thanking you. Now don't stay up all night trying to crack this case. Everything will be brought to light when the time is right."

"Did you write that little poem yourself?" I teased.

Gran scoffed. "Of course I did. One of these days Hallmark is going to pick up the card slogans I've been emailing them and your inheritance will be even sweeter!"

Just then I saw Vivian throw open the front door of Mr. Chang's, peering into the windows next door and then darting in my direction. Something was definitely up. "They're fools if they don't take note of your creative genius, Gran, there's no doubt about that. We're about ready to head home, talk to you tomorrow?"

We exchanged I-love-yous and I disconnected the call just as Vivian threw open the driver's side door, tossing a brown bag of food in my lap and giving me a maniacal look. A jolt of exhilaration shot through me. "Well, what is it?" I asked impatiently.

She grinned widely and gestured toward the adjoining restaurant. "I think we just hit the lottery."

Chapter Three - Vivian

"I can't believe this case could possibly be this easy," Parker chuckled. "Hand me one of those spring rolls, would you?"

"I can't believe my luck." I passed her the little bag with our cooling dinner in it. I'd spent exactly thirty-eight seconds earlier that afternoon planting a tracking device onto Jackson Piedmont's car, so as I waited in line for our take-out, I recognized it easily in the parking lot outside. A quick peek in the windows of the restaurant next door when I came out confirmed that it was Jackson, clearly visible sitting in the front, with a redheaded woman who was most certainly not Lisa Piedmont.

"It has to be said, if she's the mistress, she must be either an amazing conversationalist or a wildcat in bed."

I snickered. Jackson's dinner date was by no means ugly, but she was quite a bit older than him, and had that rode-hard-and-put-away-wet look to her. "If they head to a hotel after this, we can officially classify this as our easiest case to date. Did you find anything interesting on our unhappy couple?"

Parker shook her head and bit into her spring roll. "Not a thing. They're all smiles and cheery in the society pictures I found, and there's not a whisper of scandal in the gossip columns. She doesn't have a job, but everything else seems to indicate she's the picture-perfect stay-at-home wife and he's the successful architect."

"She said the problems started a few months ago, so either they're really good at hiding it, or her dates are off. Uh oh, here we go."

The waiter approached the table and handed Jackson a black folder. He glanced at it, and then tucked a few bills into it before standing and extending his hand to help the redhead up from her chair.

"No credit card trail," Parker murmured.

"Nope."

I snapped a few more pictures as the two emerged from the restaurant, exchanged goodbyes, and then went to separate cars.

"Bummer, a nice goodbye kiss would have made for a lovely exhibit at the divorce hearing." I lowered the camera and blew out my cheeks in frustration. "Who should we follow?"

Parker considered it. "You've already got him tagged, but we can just trace her by her license plate. Let's find out who she is before we waste too much time on her. She could be one of his coworkers for all we know."

"Good call." I snapped a couple of pictures of the redhead's car as she pulled away, making sure the license plate was clear and visible. Parker took the camera from me as I started my car, but Jackson didn't seem to be in a hurry to leave. He pulled out his cell phone and I cursed. "I knew I should have bugged his car when I had the chance. But with all those security cameras in the parking lot, I didn't want to risk doing it there. Slapping the tracker on was bad enough."

That was one good thing I could say about my years with the CIA...I still had a few shady contacts that could get me the more advanced technology we needed to do our job. You definitely couldn't buy it from the internet or a strip mall store.

Some of the methods Parker and I employed weren't exactly on the legal side, which technically could have cost us our license or resulted in jail time if we were caught. I suffered absolutely no crisis of conscience over it, being that the government had paid me to bribe foreign assets into committing treason for seven years. I told Parker from the beginning that if there was anything she was uncomfortable doing, she could refuse with no hard feelings, but it never seemed to bother her either. Sometimes using shady methods gave us a lead we could follow up on legally and testify to in court. So listening in on Jackson Piedmont's private phone calls wouldn't have bothered me a bit, I was just annoyed we couldn't do it at the moment.

Jackson appeared to be agitated as his phone conversation progressed. "I wonder if he's talking to Lisa?" Parker mused.

"Could be." I couldn't help but chuckle as Jackson abruptly ended the call and threw his phone onto the passenger seat, his lips clearly forming an obscenity. "Well, if it was her, he may not be going home right away."

He did drive straight home, though, with us trailing him at a safe distance. He pulled up to his gated community, and we kept going. "Well, let's go get some work done, shall we?"

~*~

"Rhiannon Simons, 1265 Lyndhurst Lane," I read out loud to Parker. Getting the redhead's information from her license plate had been child's play.

"On it," my best friend replied from her own computer, and for the next hour we were absorbed in tracking down every snippet of information about the mysterious Ms. Simons. This was when Parker and I did our best work, bouncing ideas and suggestions off each other.

"So she's a divorced insurance fraud investigator with a clean record," I said finally, after we agreed to call it a night and plopped down on the couch. "But Jackson's an architect. Why the hell would she be investigating an architectural firm? Or why would they need her?"

Parker shrugged. "Maybe she really is the girlfriend."

"Maybe, but I'm just not getting that feeling. There didn't seem to be much chemistry there. Familiarity, definitely. But no goodnight kiss or anything?"

"They were in public," Parker pointed out. "Maybe he's just smarter and more discreet than ninety-nine percent of those cheating assholes. We sure haven't found any hard evidence yet...but then again, we're just getting started."

~*~

As we'd arranged with Lisa, later that week I pecked Jackson's cell number into our shop phone. He answered almost immediately. "This is Jack Piedmont."

I made a mental note that he must go by Jack all the time, Lisa had called him that too. "Hi Mr. Piedmont! This is Vivian calling from Pistils Flower Shop, to schedule an appointment for your floral consultation!"

"Umm..." He definitely sounded confused. "I'm sorry, but I think you have the wrong number. I don't need a...a what? Floral consultation?"

"Ohhh, I'm so sorry!" I used my most contrite voice. "I assumed your wife, Lisa, told you. She wanted you to be in charge of the floral arrangements for your parents' fiftieth wedding anniversary party!"

If Jack had sounded confused before, he was downright baffled now. "Lisa wants me to be in charge of *that*?"

"Yes, she said that she's swamped with planning the final details, and completely forgot about the flowers. Luckily we were able to squeeze you in, and she said you'd know better what your parents' tastes are anyway."

"And she assumed I'd have time to do something like that?" Irritation was creeping into his voice now. "I'm sorry Miss, umm..."

"Just Vivian."

"Vivian. I don't mean to be rude to you, I really don't, but I'm a very busy man. I honestly don't have time to sit around figuring out which flowers my parents would like. I don't have a clue what they'd like, actually."

"If you like, I could just bring you some pictures of arrangements for similar parties we've done," I said encouragingly. I had to meet this guy in person, if only to get a read on him and his feelings about his wife. Getting close enough to wirelessly transmit bugging software onto his cell phone would be a bonus too.

He sighed. "I can't believe she did this...actually, yes I do. All right Vivian, can you maybe e-mail them to me?"

"We prefer to meet with you in person," I said woefully. "And you'll need to sign the invoice. But I promise not to take up any more than half an hour of your time, how's that?"

"I give up," he muttered. "I have a hole in my schedule this afternoon at 3:15, and that's the best I can do."

"That's perfect for me!" I enthused. "Thirty minutes, or maybe even less."

Jack did not share my enthusiasm. "All right, let

me give you my work address."

I already had all his information, of course, but I pretended to scratch it down anyway. "Sounds good, I'll see you then!"

"Goodbye, Vivian."

"That's the perkiest I've heard you sound in a while," Parker giggled. "You sounded like me."

"I take my lessons from the best. Sweet, I'll definitely bug his office then."

Parker handed me a glossy binder. "Here's some anniversary stuff. He'll probably just pick the first ones, but steer him toward the third theme. I'd like to do that one again."

"Will do. So what are you up to this afternoon?" Gran ran the shop for us when we were thick in the middle of a case.

"I think I'll just get some things done around here, actually. We had a few orders come in through the website a little bit ago. I'm also going to set up a meeting with Lisa for tomorrow to show her those pictures, to see if she recognizes this Rhiannon chick. If she does and can confirm she's no one to worry about, we can cross her off our to-do list."

"Okay, I'll just see you back at home then."

"Sounds good!"

~*~

Jack's architectural firm was ensconced in a

gorgeous old Savannah house, but the interior was strictly modern. I gave my name to the receptionist, and she immediately escorted me into his office. He must have really wanted to get it over with.

I knew Jack Piedmont was a good-looking guy, but up close, he was even more so. His green eyes went straight to mine and held my gaze as he shook my hand. Just the tiniest touch of gray threaded through the dark brown hair at his temples, and his handshake was warm and firm.

Quit checking out the mark, Vivian...

"Mr. Piedmont, thank you for seeing me, I'm so sorry that this was sprung on you like this."

"Please, call me Jack. And I should be apologizing to you." He gestured politely to a chair and waited for me to sit before he went back around his desk. "I'm sorry I was so rude to you earlier, that was inexcusable on my part. It's just that my wife tends to drop these things on me last-minute without considering that I might not be able to accommodate her."

"Well I won't take up a second more of your time than necessary." I smiled and handed him the binder.

He looked at the Pistils logo on the front and laughed. "Oh, I get it now. On the phone earlier, I assumed you meant *Pistols*, and I've been wondering all afternoon why in the world a flower shop would be named after a gun."

I laughed too. Good thing he didn't know it was an intentional double entendre, a joke between Parker and me. We both had handguns with concealed carry permits, not to mention the sniper rifle and the semi-automatic 9mm carbine I had locked safely away in my closet at home. Parker's Kel-Tec had custom pink grips, something I still teased her about, while my .45 Bersa was strictly business-black. Some might have called us over-cautious or downright paranoid, we considered it being prepared and protected in our field.

"Well, some people still don't get it, you know, pistils, stamens, all that. I'm impressed that you do."

"I paid attention in science class." He flashed a grin at me before flipping open the binder. "Honestly Vivian...I'm a guy. I know nothing about floral arrangements, much less ones for parties. Can you help me out here? The party isn't going to be over-the-top since my mom has put the kibosh on it being a political back-slapping extravaganza." He paused and his cheeks flushed slightly. "I'm guessing you know who my dad is?"

"Of course, Jack. And we can make it as elegant or as simple as you think your parents would prefer." I guided him to the third theme as Parker had requested. "This is one of my favorites. They'll look gorgeous in the Grantham House, we've worked there before and we're familiar with it."

He flipped through the photos, paying more

attention than I'd expected him to. "You do nice work. These look better than the flowers at my wedding."

Thank God for Parker and Gran. "We don't do too many weddings, only if they're pretty small. There are only three of us running the business, so we can't take on too much at once."

"I know the feeling, we're a small business too. Me, my partner, and three associates." He kept paging through the binder.

Just then, the alarm I'd pre-set on my phone went off, making it sound as though I had an incoming phone call. "Oh, I'm so sorry! Let me just mute that."

"No problem," he murmured.

I jabbed the mute button on the phone in my purse, grabbed the tiny bug and then quickly stuck it to the underside of his desk. It would wirelessly record and transmit the sounds in his office to my computer until either Parker or I retrieved it, after the case was over.

I straightened back up just as Jack shut the binder. "I like the ones you suggested, let's go with those. I take it Lisa hasn't paid you either?"

"No, but if you'll sign the invoice, we'll bill you." I handed the paper over to him, and he signed it neatly at the bottom.

"If you knew my wife..." he said, half to himself.

"She seemed very stressed when we met with her on Monday," I said sympathetically.

His eyebrows went up. "You met with her, and she couldn't do this then?"

"She really wanted you to be part of the planning, I think."

"That's...odd." His brow furrowed. "She usually wants me to keep my nose out of any kind of party she's planning."

I shrugged, hoping he didn't suspect anything. "Maybe because it's your parents? This was your token job?"

That got another laugh out of him. "Well, Vivian from Pistils Flower Shop, do you have a card on you? I really like what I just saw, and you do much better work than the florist we currently use for our clients. You'll be getting some business from us."

"Oh, thank you, we appreciate it!" I handed him one of my business cards and he looked at it immediately.

"Vivian Carmichael."

"My best friend teases me that I have a soap opera name. It's a bit of a mouthful."

"It's a very nice name." He tucked the card in his pocket and stood. "I'll walk you out." He put a polite hand on my back, warm through my Pistils polo. Then he opened the door for me, every inch the gentleman.

Good-looking and good manners to boot. It really made me hope that this guy wasn't a cheating asshole.

56633187R00080

Made in the USA
Middletown, DE
23 July 2019